feeling utterly ridiculous, and at the same time completely content in his arms. "I'm sorry," she said, once she trusted her voice.

"The summer's been good, hasn't it?" Nathaniel laid his cheek on the top of her head and held her tighter. "I'll miss this porch most of all."

"Me, too." She pressed her face against his chest, a fresh wave of tears rushing into her eyes. She'd sat in this very place, unloading her darkest secrets, her greatest fears, been comforted and listened, and even... The memory of Nathaniel's kiss was nearly more than she could take. Her heart felt like it was being squeezed, and she gasped for air. She took a step back, releasing her grip.

"Val?"

Swallowing against her tight throat, she raised her gaze to his.

He lifted a wet strand of hair from her face, and his gaze dropped to her lips before returning to hers.

If only she could look into those blue eyes every day, be held by him every time she cried, if only...

"Daddy! Val!"

The sound of Ruby's voice broke Val's blissful bubble. She must have gotten impatient and unbuckled her carseat.

"We're on the porch, Ruby." Nathaniel's gaze didn't leave Val's face.

Val rubbed her fingers over her cheeks one more time before hurrying to meet Ruby. She glanced back and saw Nathaniel still watching her until she rounded the side of the house.

Praise for Jennifer Moore

"Caution: Reading this sweet romance of two people of different backgrounds strengthening each other's weaknesses and appreciating their strengths will make you yearn for a beautiful beach house with a porch overlooking the ocean. *CHANGE OF HEART* left me smiling and happy. Another great book from Moore!"

~Amy Nelson

~*~

"*CHANGE OF HEART* is a fantastic read, it grabs you right from the start."

~Becky Smith

~*~

"A heart-warming story about learning to accept help and love again, we all deserve a second chance! My heart caught hold of Val and Nathaniel, cheering them on silently as I followed their journey in Jennifer Moore's beautiful tale *CHANGE OF HEART*."

~Ashley Eddy

Change of Heart

by

Jennifer Moore

The Lobster Cove Series

Change Of Heart

Cover Art by *Tina Lynn Stout*

The Wild Rose Press, Inc.
PO Box 708
Adams Basin, NY 14410-0708
Visit us at www.thewildrosepress.com

Publishing History
First Sweetheart Rose Edition, 2016
Print ISBN 978-1-5092-0665-0
Digital ISBN 978-1-5092-0666-7

The Lobster Cove Series
Published in the United States of America

Dedication

For my sister Allison
And all single parents everywhere.
Yours is the toughest job in the world,
and you do it splendidly.

Chapter One

Nathaniel ignored the buzzing in his pocket and gazed across the park where the morning sun shimmered on the waves in the harbor. He inhaled a deep breath of fresh sea air but let it out in a huff of irritation as his phone vibrated *again*. This vacation had seemed like such a good idea when he'd rented the cottage for the summer in Lobster Cove, Maine, but if his office didn't stop bothering him, this trip wouldn't be a vacation at all. He needed a change of scenery. They all did.

He finished the last sip of his coffee and threw the paper cup in the trash. He rubbed his thumb over the callous where his wedding ring had been, and the familiar guilt twisted in his stomach. Guilt that he didn't feel devastated every time he thought of Clara, guilt that what had begun as a fairy tale had become anything but. He shook off the thoughts and turned his attention to his two children, Ruby Sophia and Finn Charles, playing near the gazebo in the park by the post office.

Ruby threw bits of her muffin to the seagulls, watching as they edged their way close to snatch the pieces.

Her brother ran through the flock of birds, scattering them in a flurry of feathers and squawking. Just the thing a three year old would find entertaining.

Nathaniel's chest filled with warmth as he watched them. All the fighting with Clara, the tension, growing apart, and bitterness, he would do it over in a heartbeat because of the two beautiful children the marriage had produced. He never would have imagined he could love two people as much as he loved Ruby and Finn. The twist of guilt returned—tighter this time. He should have felt the same sentiments for his wife. Should feel empty at her loss. His phone buzzed again and this time, he answered. The marriage counselor had told him that any time his emotions became too complex to handle, he buried himself in work. She was right.

"Cavanaugh here."

"Sorry to bother you, Mr. Cavanaugh, but Mr. Knox insisted you be part of the call with Mr. Pennington." The paralegal's voice squeaked.

It should. The whiny kid had bothered Nathaniel at least five times a day since his vacation began last week. He gritted his teeth. He didn't have the patience for this. When he got back to Boston, he would address this issue with the new staff member. "Patch me in." Nathaniel stood at the edge of the park near the post office where tourists waited for the trolley. He figured it must be getting close because the group was growing.

The idea of a trolley ride and a visit to Martin Lighthouse thrilled Ruby and Finn.

And Nathaniel was determined not to let work keep him from spending a long overdue day sight-seeing with his kids.

As he listened to the conference call and made the occasional comment, he studied the people that gathered: retired couples sporting golf visors and shopping bags, families that talked excitedly and took pictures, sunburned teenagers poking at smart phones.

He wondered how many of them were just going through the motions. When his family had been together, Nathaniel had felt as if they were always pretending. In ten years, would *his* children be distant and annoyed with him? Ruby wasn't far from that attitude now. He'd hoped this vacation would change all of that. They'd reconnect and start to move past their mother's death. A fresh start. A change of scenery. After all, Clara's death had been nearly nine months ago.

A young woman caught his eye as she walked unsteadily across First Street in high stilettos that she was clearly unused to wearing.

Nathaniel tried not to stare, but found it virtually impossible. Everything about her was extreme. Her fingernails and lips were the brightest shade he'd seen on anyone, and her purse—was it made of pink fur? Her skirt was too tight, her hair too big, her blouse too low, her curves too—

Nathaniel reined in his thoughts, realizing he hadn't been paying attention to his partner and their client. He muttered something into the phone to indicate he still listened and scanned the park, locating Ruby and Finn near the gazebo.

The young woman sat on a bench in the shade of the Captain's Library and kicked off her shoes, bending and flexing her toes.

Though he stood at least twenty feet away, he could see dark red blisters forming. *Why did women insist upon wearing shoes that hurt their feet?*

Even among the tourists who didn't dress in the conservative New England style, the woman stood out.

3

She tugged on her skirt, as if she was uncomfortable, and kept checking her pink, rhinestone-encrusted watch, looking as nervous as a defendant during sentencing. He wondered if she was meeting someone. The sound of his name brought his thoughts back to the conversation. He made a flimsy excuse about his wireless connection as his mind scrambled to come up with something to say to reassure his client that he had matters well in hand. Even though he didn't.

Nathaniel wondered again why he thought he could leave Boston for the summer and work remotely from the little office in the vacation cottage. He rested his hand in the crook of his elbow, pressing his arm tight against his chest and shifted from one foot to the other. His stress level rose.

Finn ran past, squealing as seagulls flapped frantically to get out of his way.

As she watched him, the woman on the bench smiled.

Nathaniel had to admit she had a lovely smile, and if her face wasn't covered in an entire rainbow of make-up, she would be quite attractive. The thought surprised him. He'd definitely been alone too long.

After a moment, she checked her tacky glittering watch again and slipped her feet back into her shoes, wincing as she stood. She brushed her hands over the back of her skirt and shouldered her furry purse. She started walking then hesitated, changing her path slightly to step off the curb.

Nathaniel figured she must have decided to cross the street since the crowd waiting for the trolley blocked the sidewalk.

The group shifted. The trolley must be

approaching.

Nathaniel looked around to gather his children. He called and waved to Ruby who joined him right away. Where was Finn?

Birds screeched. Nathaniel snapped his gaze in their direction just as Finn jumped off the curb and chased the squawking seagulls into the street. Pain compressed his gut, and Nathaniel choked on his breath. Finn was directly in the path of the trolley!

****

Val looked up the street toward The Venus Gallery, feeling a rush of nerves. As she clicked-clacked across the road, she again cursed her choice of shoes. Her feet were killing her. She glanced down at her watch—even though she'd checked the time just a few seconds earlier. She was five minutes early for her job interview. *Perfect timing.* She wanted to appear prompt and reliable, but not desperate. A flock of birds flapped past in a rush startling her, and Val glanced back, hearing the ringing of the trolley bell.

The dark-haired boy she'd watched in the park jumped off the curb behind her and ran after them. At the rate the trolley was moving, there was no way the boy would avoid getting hit.

Val felt her muscles tingle as panic shot through them. People in the crowd screamed and pointed, but Val was the only one close enough to do anything. She whirled, dropped her purse, and pulled up her tight skirt a few inches, darting in front of the trolley. Her heel caught in the tracks, and she stumbled. She lifted the boy into her arms as the trolley brakes screeched. She wasn't fast enough to avoid the slow-moving, but heavy, vehicle. It slammed into her left hip and spun her, throwing her across the ground. Val held the boy against her tightly, absorbing the shock of the impact. Burning pain shot up her leg as she took the brunt of the skid on her right elbow and thigh.

Once she stopped sliding, Val righted herself into a sitting position, blinking for a moment, her thoughts fuzzy. The realization she held a sobbing child made her instantly alert. She leaned her lower back against the curb and examined the boy to make sure he hadn't been hurt.

He appeared unharmed, only scared. She brushed the tears from his cheeks. "Hey, buddy, you're all right."

The man she assumed to be the boy's father ran toward her, followed by the trolley driver, a little girl, and a whole group of curious onlookers—some of whom snapped pictures of the scene.

The father knelt and placed his hand on the boy's back. His face was chalky and his jaw clenched. "Finn, are you hurt?" He turned to Val. "Is he hurt? Are you…"

His gaze moved to her elbow, and then down, she assumed, to her thigh.

His lips pulled back in a slight grimace. He tried to lift the boy, but he, *Finn?*, clung to Val and buried his face against her chest. Daddy looked from the boy to Val. "You may need a doctor." He pulled out his phone, tapping the screen.

Val assumed he sent a text.

"My friend works at the clinic just down the street." His phone buzzed, and he glanced down at the screen again. "He's on his way."

Val held onto Finn while she twisted her arm,

tipping her head to take a better look at her stinging elbow. Her skin was raw and bleeding. Pieces of gravel were imbedded in deeper scrapes. She leaned around the boy, and although she couldn't see much with him sitting on her lap, she got enough of a glimpse to see her thigh was in the same condition. Val sucked in a breath through her teeth. Now that the adrenaline was wearing off, pain throbbed through her injuries. She shook her head. "It's just a little road rash."

"The injuries look worse than that." His brows pinched together. "I—"

"You saw them jump out in front of me." The sputtering trolley driver cut in. "There was no way I could have stopped in time. I have all these witnesses."

The trolley driver stood in the way of a police officer as he pled his case.

Val squinted at the men. *Does he really think the cop can't see us?*

The police officer stepped around the trolley driver and knelt next to Val. He moved his gaze quickly over her and Finn. "I'm Officer Harris. Can you tell me your name, miss?"

"Val McKinley."

Daddy knelt on her other side. "I contacted Seth Goodwyn," he told Officer Harris. "He'll be here soon."

The officer glanced at him and nodded, and then turned his attention back to Val. "Miss McKinley, just relax. A doctor's on the way."

"I don't need a doctor, sir, thank you." Although she knew he was just doing his job, Val's frustration grew "Once I'm certain that Finn is calmed down, I'll need to get going. I have an appointment."

Officer Harris glanced over his shoulder at the commotion the trolley driver created. "Sit tight, Miss McKinley. I need to take care of this." He excused himself and walked toward the trolley driver.

Finn's father placed his hand on his son's back. "You're all right now. Seth is coming." He spoke in a soft voice, but the boy did not release his hold on Val.

Val closed her eyes against the pain that spread like fire over her skin.

As he spoke to the officer, the trolley driver moved again, blocking the view of Val and Finn while he told his story. His voice rose, and along with the increase in volume, it became higher and squeaky.

Witnesses argued about where they had been and what they had seen.

The police officer put out his hands to quiet them. "Listen, we'll get to all your testimonies soon enough. I've got a deputy on the way who would love to listen to each and every one of you. But right now, I'm gonna need you to cooperate. So, everybody, back up."

In spite of Officer Harris' warning, the trolley driver continued his diatribe.

The officer raised his voice again.

Finn's crying, which had been nearly calmed, started once more and despite his father's comforting words, he buried his face against her neck.

Val's body temperature rose along with her headache. She'd had enough of these bickering men. *Can't they see they're upsetting Finn?* "Do y'all mind?" Val said in a loud voice.

The men stopped arguing and turned.

"Take it somewhere else." She jerked up her chin. "This boy is scared enough without having to listen to y'all fighting like stray cats in an alley."

The officer and trolley driver moved a bit away, ducking their heads as they walked.

Val turned her attention back to Finn, murmuring, "There we go. They'll be quiet now." She kicked off her stilettos. The leather had torn off of the heel of one when she caught it in the trolley tracks. The sight made her stomach sink. She'd loved those shoes, even though they were a half-size too small.

The young girl Val had seen earlier stood behind her father, wide eyed. "Your skirt is ripped," she said.

Val hadn't even noticed her skirt. Again, she twisted to the side and shifted Finn so she could see the full extent of the damage. *Great.* The tight skirt had nearly torn completely up one side and the thin fabric had done little to protect her thigh and rear end from the asphalt. Now she'd have to return to her apartment, clean up, and change outfits before she went to the gallery. That would take at least two hours. Beside the fact that the shoes and skirt from the sale rack in a local consignment store had cost a huge chunk of her savings. And now, both were ruined.

She looked around for her purse and spotted it near the tracks. *If I could just call the gallery...*but she didn't want to move and dislodge the boy from her lap. Besides, if she stood, her rear end would be in full view of everyone on the street.

"And I can see your panties." The girl pointed, hiding a smile behind her hand.

"Ruby!" Her father's face reddened. "That is certainly not appropriate."

"I appreciate it, Miss Ruby." Val smiled to let her know she wasn't offended. "Us girls need to stick

9

together, and tell each other when our panties are showing." She shifted again, searching for a position that didn't hurt or show more of her underwear, while still maintaining her hold on Finn. She scooted up awkwardly onto the curb, resting all of her weight on the side of her rear that wasn't churned up like road kill. As she moved, her other hip started to throb in the spot where the trolley had struck her. An ugly bruise was probably forming. She scowled. Waiting for a bruise to fade and the scrapes on her leg to heal would keep her from lying out on the beach anytime soon. And she had a hot pink bikini to debut.

Daddy moved from his squatting position to sit next to her on the curb.

He smelled delicious. Sort of a warm, rum-spice smell. Certainly not something he got out of a sample bin at the drugstore.

"I can't begin to thank you, Miss McKinley. I don't know what I would have done if you…" He took off his sunglasses and pressed his finger and thumb into the corners of his eyes.

"No thanks necessary. I'm glad I was close enough to help." She tried to keep her voice light, though she felt like screaming from the stabbing pain.

He turned toward her and, for just an instant, their gazes locked.

Val was startled by the color. She had never seen such deep blue eyes, and she forced away her gaze, certain the turmoil of the last few minutes was responsible for the increase in her heart rate.

Ruby stepped behind them and sat on Val's other side. "When you say *I*, it sounds like *ah*. I like how you talk."

Val was glad for an excuse to turn her attention in the girl's direction. "Why thank you, Miss Ruby. What a nice thing to say."

"I'm glad you saved Finn. And I'm sorry your bottom got hurt."

Val smiled at the girl's serious expression. "It's hard to be a big sister, isn't it? I bet y'all worry about Finn just like I worry about my brothers." Now that her brothers were both teenagers, she worried about them even more. Who knew what sort of trouble those guys were causing without Val keeping an eye on them?

Ruby knitted her eyebrows together and nodded. "I worry Finn is going to get hurt. Or in trouble."

"Finn's lucky he's got you to look out for him. Watching over your brother will make you a good momma one day."

"My mother died." Ruby clasped her hands between her knees.

That did a lot to explain why Finn was still clinging. Val's throat tightened. "I'm sorry, Ruby. My momma died, too."

Ruby sat quietly for a moment, staring at the road. Then she scrunched her nose and tipped her head to the side. "Val's a boy's name."

Out of the corner of her eye, Val saw Daddy shift his position. "People call me Val, but my real name is Valdosta." She spoke quickly before Ruby's manners were corrected again.

"That's pretty."

"Thank you. I think Ruby is a pretty name."

Finn lifted his head and scooted around on Val's lap so that he faced his sister. "And Finn is a pretty name, too."

Ruby shook her head. "Not pretty, handsome."

Daddy excused himself to speak to the officer.

Val hadn't realized how tense she'd been while he sat next to her. Now that he was gone, she relaxed. Kids she could talk to. She glanced up and took the opportunity to study him while he spoke with the other men, observing him objectively as she would a painting. His dark hair was cut short, but she thought if he allowed it to grow, he would have curls like his children. The sun revealed light caramels and deep bronze. His shoulders were square, his jaw was strong, and he had a cleft in his chin. He stood straight and confident, small lines fanning out from the corners of his eyes as he concentrated on the men's conversation.

If she were to do an artistic rendering, she would choose to paint him against the background of the sea to emphasize his deep blue eyes. She quickly looked away when she saw him watching her. *Of course, he is watching me.* She was a bloodied stranger sitting on a curb with his children. He wasn't *watching her*. Time to get real.

A blond man in a golf shirt and shorts strode up the street. He spotted the men and hurried toward them.

The children's father looked up and his face relaxed as he moved away from the others to meet the man. "Thanks for coming so quickly."

The blond man nodded and placed his hand on Finn's daddy's shoulder as he listened to what Val figured was a re-telling of the accident. His brows furrowed as he glanced toward the small group sitting on the curb.

After a quick discussion, the man walked toward Val and Finn and knelt on the street in front of them.

"I'm Dr. Goodwyn." He smiled at Val, straight white teeth against tanned skin. "*Seth* Goodwyn. Rules say you don't have to call me doctor unless I'm wearing a white coat." He winked and turned to Finn. "How ya doing, kiddo?"

Seth couldn't have been much older than thirty, and between the casual way he dressed and the bleached blond hair, she thought he looked more like a surfer than a doctor. Val glanced at Finn's daddy while Dr. Goodwyn talked to the boy.

His attention was on his son.

The concern on his face made her want to reassure him Finn was fine. But she remained silent, knowing the doctor would calm any worries better than she could. She glanced away, moving her attention to the buildings up the street. To The Venus Gallery.

She looked at her watch and winced. Now she was officially late for her appointment with Abigail Longley and would have to reschedule. "Ruby, do you think you could run and grab my purse for me?" She pointed to where she'd dropped it, near the trolley tracks. Val could only hope her phone had made it out of the accident in better shape than she had. She could never afford to buy a new one.

The doctor asked Val about the accident and checked her elbow. He crouched down to examine the scrapes on the back of her upper thigh.

Val twisted awkwardly to give him a better view of her injury. Pain shot a fiery path up her leg. She wasn't thrilled with the entire street watching while her backside was on display. As if he could read her mind, the children's father motioned Ruby toward him, and the two moved to a position that blocked the crowd's

13

view and gave Val a bit of privacy.

She tried to think of something to distract her from the doctor's examination. The wind blew, and Val shook her hair out of her face, moving carefully so she didn't disturb Finn. If it weren't for the constant sea breeze, the humidity would be sticking her hair to her neck like it did back home in West Virginia. Typically she wore a pony tail, but last night, she'd slept with her hair rolled in strips of paper towels and teased it until looked like a rodeo queen's. If that didn't impress The Venus Gallery, she didn't know what would.

Seth helped her into a more comfortable position. "I don't think you'll need stitches, but I'd like you to come into the office to get these abrasions cleaned out. And just as a precaution, I'll want to get you started on some antibiotics."

Daddy handed him a blanket someone must have donated to the cause.

Val maneuvered Finn while Seth arranged the blanket over her lap to cover her exposed leg. He pulled it tighter on her other side, and she flinched and sucked in a quick breath.

Seth's eyebrows rose. "Is this where the trolley hit you?" He indicated her left hip.

Val pursed her lips and nodded. This doctor was thoughtful and she didn't want to be rude, but she had to get moving in order to convince Abigail Longley she hadn't just blown off her interview.

If things didn't work out with The Venus Gallery, she'd need to find a gallery or an art shop in another town. The idea saddened her. In just a few days, Val had come to love the New England coast. But she wasn't looking for just any job. She needed one that would give her experience in her field of Art History. The last thing she wanted to do was limp back to Millford Creek, penniless, and return to her old job at the cigarette filter factory.

The doctor squatted back on his heels. "We'll definitely want to do some x-rays."

"I can tell ya right now, that won't be necessary. Nothing's broken."

Ruby handed Val her purse and sat next to her on the curb again.

"Much obliged, Miss Ruby." Val reached inside, pulling out her phone.

The doctor rested his forearms on his knees. "There are other things to worry about aside from fractures. I really would feel better if you were examined thoroughly. If it's me you're not comfortable with, other doctors at the clinic can—"

"My unwillingness has nothing to do with you, sir."

"Seth."

"Seth." Val nodded and smiled. "I know I'm not hurt bad enough to need a doctor, and I don't want to waste anyone's time."

"It's hardly a waste of time to make sure you're taken care of, Val."

"Well, you make a good argument. But honestly…" Val's gaze slid from his and she lowered her voice. "I can't afford a doctor." She didn't know if she'd even stretch her funds far enough for bus fare back and forth from her apartment a few more times. The small room she'd found outside of Bar Harbor had required a first and last month's rent deposit. Real estate prices in coastal New England were astronomical compared to rural West Virginia. Plus now she was worried about finding—and affording—a new skirt.

"Of course, I'll cover any medical costs." Handsome daddy stood behind Seth with his hands in his pockets.

"That's not necessary." Val lifted her gaze to meet his before lowering it again. Her face heated.

Seth tipped his head to catch her eye. "I'm sure we can figure out—"

Val drew in a deep breath. She'd pussy-footed around long enough. *Time to be assertive.* "I do appreciate your concern, but this isn't my first scraped leg. I'm not in shock, I didn't hit my head, and I know how to use hydrogen peroxide. Oh, and did I mention, I can be stubborn as a polecat once I've made up my mind?" Val gave Seth a pleasant smile that she hoped conveyed "it's not you, it's me," and opened her phone. "Excuse me a moment, will ya? I need to place a call, and then I'll finish explaining all the reasons why I don't need a doctor." She continued to rub Finn's back as she scrolled to the number for The Venus Gallery and pressed Call. Then braced herself for a conversation with Abigail Longley, the gallery owner.

Chapter Two

Seth stood and joined Nathaniel. He put his hands in his pockets and rocked back on his heels. "Finn looks fine. You could bring him in if you want, but I don't think he needs more than a good nap. Maybe give him a little children's pain reliever if he feels achy in the next few days."

Nathaniel glanced at the children sitting with the woman on the curb. He was surprised how well Val McKinley had managed to calm his son. She'd even placated Ruby, who he'd have expected to be in hysterics by now. Nathaniel lifted his chin toward Finn. "Looks like he's getting a good nap."

Finn's eyes were closed and his head lay against Val's chest.

Seth smirked and lifted his shoulders. "Kids have all the luck, don't they?"

Nathaniel didn't answer. He turned slightly in the other direction to give Val privacy as she spoke on the phone. He didn't intend to eavesdrop, but he couldn't help but hear her side of the phone conversation.

"Yes, ma'am. I know you expected me at ten o'clock, but... No, I don't make it a habit to be unreliable. If you will just let me reschedule... I...Please, if..." Her voice cut off abruptly.

Assuming the conversation had ended, Nathaniel glanced over his shoulder.

Val lowered the phone and stared at the ground.

Finn shuddered in his sleep, and Val rested her cheek on his head.

Seth excused himself and moved farther up the road to speak to Officer Harris.

"Are you sad, Val?" Ruby placed her hand on Val's arm and leaned around to see her face.

Nathaniel saw Val smile, but noticed her expression had lost most of its light.

"Just a little bit, but I'll be fine. I just need to do some thinking is all." Val rubbed her forehead.

"My daddy is taking us to Martin Lighthouse today. Have you seen the lighthouse?"

Val nodded and after a deep breath, her smile returned. She turned her knees slightly toward Ruby. "I *did* see the lighthouse. Are you climbing up all the way to the top?"

Nathaniel walked toward Officer Harris and Seth. His mind churned. From what he heard of the conversation, he concluded the accident had cost Val the opportunity for a job. He wondered where she was interviewing, and what she would do now. An idea began to form in his mind.

His gaze focused on the children, Nathaniel listened to the trolley driver, Seth, and Officer Harris as they discussed the accident. He didn't dare move too far away while a person he didn't know tended to his children, but he needed to understand how the legalities were being handled. The majority of his attention, however, was focused on the woman sitting on the curb with his children. He'd rarely seen Ruby and Finn so comfortable with someone they'd just met. Finn slept peacefully, curled up on her lap while Val gently rubbed her hand up and down his back.

Val said something to Ruby, and his daughter laughed.

The sound had become far too rare as of late. Nathaniel certainly couldn't make Ruby laugh like that. He couldn't seem to even find the right words to say.

The officer nodded occasionally as he recorded the trolley driver's statement in a small notebook.

Officer Harris seemed to be doing a thorough job in his questioning. Nathaniel would, of course, need to speak to both men when they were finished. He caught Seth's eye and saw the doctor's nod. He must have reported the extent of the injuries to the officer. He motioned with his head to the side, and Seth walked with him back toward Val and the children.

Based on his initial impression of Miss McKinley…Val. Valdosta—*What in the world kind of name is that anyway?* Nathaniel would never have imagined that within moments of laying eyes on the woman, he would nearly break down in tears of gratitude for her actions. The conflicting feelings were uncomfortable when he realized how quickly he had dismissed her because of her appearance. And now he owed her his son's life.

Instead of analyzing his emotions further, he spoke to Seth. "Do you mind taking Ruby to Julie's for a sugar cookie? I want to talk to Val for a moment."

Seth raised his brows but agreed. He took Ruby's hand and led her up the street to the sweet shop.

Nathaniel sat on the curb next to Val.

She winced as she shifted her position to face him.

He definitely needed to convince her to get medical care. "Miss McKinley, I didn't mean to listen to your conversation, but I couldn't help but overhear you had a job interview today?"

"Y'all didn't think I got dressed up to the nines to go to the beach, did ya?" Val's smile fell flat, and she let out a breath through her nose. "I had an interview at The Venus Gallery." She waved her hand toward the corner behind him, farther up the street. "I'm an art historian."

Hearing her declaration, Nathaniel fought a smile. He covered it by looking over his shoulder to the gallery. "And you missed this opportunity because of...what happened today?"

Val pursed her lips.

She was obviously troubled about offending him by admitting that he'd guessed the truth. She must not want him to feel like the missed appointment was his fault. Nathaniel could tell he was making her uncomfortable. "I'd like you to work for me."

Val squinted as she studied him. "It's real nice of you, but unless you own an art shop, a museum, or gallery, I'll keep looking. I'm hoping to travel to Paris for an internship, and a job in my field will help my application. I do appreciate the offer, though."

"I was actually hoping I could convince you to be my nanny." He shook his head, still surprised by the abruptness of his decision. "I mean Ruby and Finn's nanny."

"A nanny? Like Mary Poppins?" Her brows rose, revealing even more colors in her rainbow of eye makeup. "I don't even know you, and you don't know me from Adam. How can you be sure I don't have a criminal record?"

He straightened. "Do you?"

"Of course not." Her lips twisted. "Unless you count the time me and my friends were caught skinny-dippin' in the high school pool." She waved a hand. "But I was a minor, and they told me it's been expunged."

This was undoubtedly the most bizarre interview he'd ever conducted, but to his credit, he usually had time to prepare. He'd rarely made such a quick decision and wasn't quite sure how to approach this. *Time to get back on track.* "Listen, Miss McKinley…"

"Call me Val."

"Val, I'm sorry, I'm a little shaken today. I'm going about this in the wrong order. First of all, I should have introduced myself." He twisted to face her and extended his hand. "My name is Nathaniel Cavanaugh."

Val's arms were still wrapped around sleeping Finn, but she shifted and grasped his hand with her left. "Pleased to meet you." She squeezed his fingers.

"Val, I could call an agency and weed through applications, and then interview someone, that I could only hope my kids even remotely like *and* who's willing to move up here for the summer. But that could take weeks. You're here now, and you seem to click with them, and I really need help. We're just here for a few months, and—"

Val held up her hand. "Listen, you don't owe me anything. It's not your fault, or Finn's, that I missed the appointment. An accident's an accident. Maybe things were meant to be this way, and a perfect job is waiting for me in a town I've never heard of. I really do appreciate ya looking out for me, but I won't take a job offered out of guilt or charity." She brushed Finn's

21

curls off his forehead and pulled back her shoulders, dipping her chin to see the boy's face. She smiled at Nathaniel. "I do think your kids are pretty wonderful. If I didn't need an art job, I'd have a hard time turning you down."

Nathaniel wasn't above begging. He couldn't wait for weeks—he needed someone now, and that someone had practically fallen into his lap. Or crash-landed in a mess of blood and cheap eye shadow. Either way, he wasn't used to losing. He opened his mouth to deliver a counter-argument.

Officer Harris squatted down in front of them. "Miss McKinley, I'll take your statement, and you'll need to fill out an accident report. But it can wait until after you've gone into the clinic. Doc says you need medical care."

Val narrowed her eyes and pushed out a breath. "How about I just tell ya everything right now? Get it done and we can all get going. The telling's not complicated." She shifted Finn to her other shoulder and sat straight. "Finn didn't see the trolley, and I grabbed him before he could get hit. Thanks to my stupid shoes, I wasn't fast enough to get us both out of the way in time, and I ended up with some road rash. That's the whole thing, cut and dry. File it or write it up, or do whatever y'all do with it." She waved her hand through the air, brushing away the entire incident.

Nathaniel shook his head. "Val, don't be too hasty. There's still a lot to be done. You should document facts to possibly file a case later. You'll need the vehicle maintenance history for the trolley, the driver's record, and police report. Also, you should probably talk to the municipal authority that runs public transportation. Get all your ducks in a row."

Val turned slowly to face him. She lowered her chin and pulled it back against her neck, squinting her eyes. "Now, why in the world would I do all that? So I can sue someone and ruin his life?"

Nathaniel kept his voice calm, as if he were speaking to a child. This was a topic he knew well. "Gathering facts isn't about suing, or ruining lives. It's about duty and causation."

"You sound like a lawyer." Val shook her head. "I don't need a lawyer any more than I need a doctor. I *do* need to get going." She turned to Officer Harris. "If we're finished here, my butt feels like someone took a weed whacker to it, and my clothes are shredded. You have my phone number, and if you think of any other questions, call me. I'm leaving town tomorrow and—"

"Where are you going, Val?" Ruby's voice sounded close to tears.

Nathaniel turned to see his daughter and Seth standing behind him. Ruby's brow was furrowed.

Val's shoulders slumped. "Well, that's what I need to figure out, Miss Ruby. First of all, though, I need a shower, don't you think?"

Ruby held out a small paper bag. "I brought you a cookie."

Val smiled softly as Ruby handed her the paper sack. She opened the bag and took out a lobster-shaped sugar cookie. "Thank you. How did you know I love cookies?" She took a bite, dropping crumbs onto Finn's head.

Ruby laughed.

Val licked the frosting from the corner of her mouth and winked. "Now don't ya wake him up, or he's gonna want our cookies."

"It's okay. I brought one for Finn, too."

"My, Ruby, however did you get to be so thoughtful?" Val shook her head.

She acted as if bringing a child a cookie was an act of the greatest charity she could imagine.

Ruby's eyes shined at the praise.

How does she do that? He praised his kids all the time, and Ruby never looked at him that way. Nathaniel squirmed inside. His kids were smart. They knew when a compliment was genuine and not just an effort to build their positive self-worth by following *The Affirmative Nurturing Parenting Handbook.* He gritted his teeth, his determination renewed. There had to be a way to convince Val to stay, if he could only find something she couldn't refuse. His gaze fell on Ruby, and he smiled to himself. Finding people's weaknesses and exploiting them was a particular specialty of his.

****

Val's head pounded. Her elbow and the back of her thigh had progressed from stinging to a painful burn, and her bruised hip throbbed. She didn't think she could sit, balanced uncomfortably on this hard curb, holding a sleeping child and smiling as if everything were just peachy-keen, for much longer. She was ready to leave.

"If y'all will excuse me, I really should get going." She lifted Finn gently away and shifted him into Nathaniel's arms. She brushed the curls off the boy's forehead again as he settled against his father. After holding Finn for so long, Val shivered at the cool breeze.

"Since you're not coming into the clinic, can I at least check on you tomorrow?" Seth touched her arm to recapture her attention.

"Like I told ya, I'll be gone tomorrow." Val tried to smooth the wrinkles that had been smashed into her shirt by the warm little body, but wondered after a moment why she bothered. A pressed blouse would hardly make a difference in her appearance. Her skirt was barely held together by a polyester waistband.

"I can call you." He pulled a phone out of his pocket.

"Sure." Val smiled, even though her headache was making her nauseous. "If it makes you feel better." She gave him her number then stood and swayed slightly.

Officer Harris and Seth both took a hold of an arm.

"Steady." Seth's brows were pinched together. "Maybe you should sit back down."

Val forced a laugh, hoping they couldn't tell how sick she felt. "I stood up too quick." She pulled the blanket tighter and held the corners together in front of her waist.

"Where did you park? I'll get you to your car." Officer Harris released her arm.

"I took the bus. The station's not far." Val bent down and picked up her purse and shoes. The devil himself wouldn't convince her to put those torture devices back on her feet. She straightened, making the head rush return, and she closed her eyes against the spell of dizziness.

"We'll drive you home." Nathaniel stood, shifting Finn carefully to his shoulder to keep him from waking. "Ruby, will you hold Val's hand? She looks pale."

Val met Nathaniel's innocent-looking gaze with a smirk. She knew what he was doing. She wouldn't be manipulated by her soft spot for his kids, but she could use the ride. The very idea of walking to the bus station, and then from the Bar Harbor station to her apartment made her want to sit back down on the curb and cry.

"Take it easy tonight, Val." Seth's expression was still wary as he glanced at her elbow. "Make sure you get those scrapes cleaned well, and pick up some antibacterial ointment. Take some ibuprofen. You'll be hurting tomorrow. And if the pain in your hip gets any worse, don't hesitate to go to an emergency room. Understand?"

"Got it. Thanks, Seth."

Seth waved and walked back down the road toward the clinic.

"Our car's just across the street in the grocery store parking lot." Nathaniel walked a little ahead. He glanced back as he led them through the cars.

At a slower pace, Val and Ruby followed. Val held the blanket corners and her shoes in one hand, and Ruby clutched the other.

"We like to get breakfast at Sweet Bea's." Ruby pointed across the park at the bakery. "Do you like blueberry muffins?"

"Course I do." Val tried to keep her voice cheerful as she concentrated on walking in a straight line and not jostling her pounding head.

"What did you have for breakfast?"

The last thing Val wanted to think about right now was food. "A lobster cookie."

Nathaniel turned his head slightly.

"A cookie isn't a nutritious meal." Ruby spoke in a scolding voice.

"You're right. I should have eaten healthier. I was in a hurry this morning."

Nathaniel clicked his key fob to unlock the doors of a silver luxury sedan. He carefully set Finn into his car seat, attaching the straps around the sleeping boy, and then opened the passenger door for Val.

"Thanks." She grimaced as she sat back into the seat and looked up quickly to see if he had noticed.

Nathaniel's eyes narrowed. "We'll be right back." He took Ruby's hand and walked into the grocery mart.

Val leaned her head back against the seat and closed her eyes. Now that she was alone, she allowed herself to shudder at the pain in her body and fully feel the weight of her discouragement. Tears itched behind her eyes, and she took a few deep breaths to calm herself. Bawling wouldn't solve anything. She would feel better once she cleaned up and took some pain medicine—and a nap. Then she'd have a clear mind to figure out her next move.

It seemed like just a moment later that Val heard the click of the door opening. She wasn't sure whether they had returned quickly. Or maybe she had fallen asleep. She wiped at her eyes, making sure no traces of her pity party were evident.

Nathaniel helped Ruby into her seat and climbed behind the wheel. He handed a grocery bag and a bottle of water to Val.

She opened the bag and took out a package of ibuprofen, a tube of antibacterial ointment, an apple, and a deli sandwich. Val raised her eyebrows.

"Ruby wanted to make sure you ate a nutritious lunch." He adjusted the mirror and pulled onto the road.

Val turned to look into the back seat, nearly gasping at the pain in her bruised hip when she twisted. "Thank you, Ruby." She sat forward in the seat again and directed a pointed look at Nathaniel. "Maybe Daddy shouldn't use his daughter's thoughtfulness as a tool."

"I'm used to getting what I want." The corner of his lips pulled.

"And that makes two of us." She narrowed her eyes.

"Tell me, Val, where are you from?" Nathaniel said when they reached the main road leading from Lobster Cove.

She eyed him, not trusting the harmless question. "West Virginia. Millford Creek. I bet y'all never heard of it."

"It's true. I haven't." He adjusted the air conditioner and put a finger on the vent aiming at her. "How's the temperature?"

The cool air helped with her nausea, even though it stung her scrapes. "Just fine, thanks."

He nodded and moved his hand to rest on his leg. "So what brings you so far from home?"

Val leaned her head back against the seat to keep the headache under control as she talked. "A professor of mine recommended Bar Harbor. She had a friend with an art gallery and thought it would be a great place for me to get some experience before applying for the Paris internship. But when I got there, I found that the friend had moved away and sold her gallery."

"Didn't you contact her before you made the trip all the way up here?"

She resented the look of disapproval in his face. Of course she had already beaten herself up a hundred times for not planning out the situation better. "I only had her name and the gallery's address."

"But you could have looked her up, maybe done a little research on the place?"

Val felt her defenses rise. She didn't like the insinuation that she hadn't thought this through. "I took a trip to the campus library to use the internet and found the gallery's website. It hadn't been updated in a while. Looking back, that should have been a red flag, but I saw all the galleries and art shops in Bar Harbor, and I guess I just figured one of them had to work out."

"You tried them all?"

Val glanced sideways and nodded. Her cheeks felt hot, but she figured she had nothing to lose by telling the truth. "I apparently don't project the sort of image people look for when they come into a high-end gallery." She hoped the sarcasm in her voice masked the hurt she still felt at being rejected so often. Those precise words had been spoken by a trendy, spiky haired gallery owner as she looked Val up and down through her tortoise shell glasses. Val hadn't realized how strong her accent was until the woman pointed it out, or how unfashionable her clothing looked. "One docent recommended I try The Venus Gallery in Lobster Cove, and I hoped getting dolled up and buying a new outfit to look more professional would change my luck. But, I guess The Venus Gallery wasn't meant to be." She shrugged, looking out the window.

The car followed the road down the coast, and Val watched as a boat full of tourists headed out of the harbor—no doubt hoping to see whales, seals, and puffins along the rocky shoreline. They lifted cameras and phones as the vessel passed Martin Lighthouse, and Val imagined if she had been aboard, she'd have heard cameras clicking. She'd certainly taken her fair share of pictures when she rode the ferry to Lobster Cove the day before. The ferry ride had been a splurge. Just another of her bad decisions as far as managing her money. She was about an inch away from broke and had left home less than a week earlier.

She decided they'd talked about her quite enough. "And where are y'all from? You said you're just here for the summer…"

"Boston."

"Are you a lawyer in Boston?"

Nathaniel nodded. He glanced at her and then turned back to the road, his fingers drumming on the steering wheel. "I take it from your tone, you're not overly fond of attorneys?"

That was an understatement if she'd ever heard one. "I just don't trust them."

His eyebrows shot up.

The action was no doubt because of her bluntness. "Nothing personal." She was glad she'd stopped before she mentioned the words "thieving varmints" or "lying snakes." She didn't want to offend this man when he had been generous enough to drive her home. Time to change the subject—pronto. "Ruby, are you going to school when you get back to Boston?" Val turned her head to look into the back seat.

Ruby had fallen asleep with her cheek leaning on her hand.

Val glanced to her brother and smiled at how adorable both children looked. She settled back in her seat gingerly as her leg throbbed. "Looks like you get a quiet ride home."

When the car neared Bar Harbor, she directed him away from the main town, through the outer neighborhoods, and finally to the nearly deserted street where she'd found the only apartment within ten miles that she could afford.

Nathaniel lowered his head to look up at the building through his windshield.

"I appreciate the ride." Val reached for the door handle. "And tell Ruby and Finn 'bye' for me. Y'all are lucky to have such good kids."

"Val, wait."

She let her arm drop and blew out a sigh. "I know what you're about to say. But I really can't do it."

"I am willing to negotiate. I'll lay all my cards on the table." He shifted into Park and pulled the brake, turning toward her. "The thing is, we need this vacation. The kids, Ruby especially, have had a hard time since their mother died, and I haven't known how to connect with them. I thought a summer in Maine would be the perfect thing. But I underestimated how much work was needed to entertain two children full time and still keep up with the demands of my job. I can't do it alone. I need help, and not just any help. I need someone who will love my kids, and I'm willing to do just about anything at this point to get you to stay."

Val folded her arms. "I'm not playing hard ball with ya. I really can't." She twisted toward him as far as she could without pulling on her scraped leg or straining her bruised hip. "So, I'll lay my cards on the table, too." She looked at him, and then turned her gaze out the window. "I basically raised my brothers and sisters after my momma died, and then I worked two jobs to keep us afloat when my daddy was laid off. Me going to college was a big sacrifice for all of us." She glanced up.

He nodded, indicating for her to continue.

"I took on extra hours and saved every single penny that didn't go to the mortgage or food. My schooling took nearly six years, since I could only squeeze in a few classes at a time, and the community college campus was an hour and a half from our town. But once I got that degree, I saw how proud my family was." Her eyes misted, and she fought down the wave of homesickness that she'd never felt before.

"Nobody in our little town had gone to college. My daddy insisted that I apply for Paris. His new job gives him better hours, the trailer's almost paid for, and he practically pushed me out the door." She swallowed and looked across the seat at him. "Mr. Cavanaugh, your kids are great, really. I can't think of many things I'd rather do than spend the summer with them, but I can't let down my family. I've already made about a hundred mistakes, and I've only been gone a week, I have to do this, to follow my dream, because it's their dream, too. Do ya see what I'm saying?"

Nathaniel studied her for a moment. He squinted his eyes and ran his thumbnail over his bottom lip. "I think I have an idea that will help both of us."

Val opened her mouth to object.

He held up his hand. "Just hear me out, okay?"

She nodded and pursed her lips. He wasn't used to being told no.

"How much is a plane ticket to Paris?"

"Fifteen hundred dollars."

"Sounds about right." He nodded. "So, I'll pay you fifteen hundred in cash right off the bat. You come out and stay at our vacation cottage, all expenses included.

You'll have a car for your use, one day off per week in addition to holidays, money for taking Ruby and Finn on excursions, and I'll pay you twice what I paid our nanny in Boston."

Val's mouth went dry at the amount of money he offered. In three months, she'd make more than she made in a year back home. She squeezed her eyes shut and breathed in and out. She needed to focus. If she wrote home and told her family that she'd left them all to move up north and be a babysitter…How could she disappoint them like that? They were so proud of her. She held on to the memory of her father bragging to the guys down at Lucas Drugstore about his daughter going to Paris and being a "real historian with a degree to prove it." She opened her eyes and shook her head, wishing she hadn't when the pain increased. "I'm sorry—"

"Oh, perhaps I forgot to mention one of my fraternity brothers is married to an assistant curator of the Museum of Fine Arts in Boston. And he owes me a favor. I'll place a call today." He flipped one hand over as he spoke. "You work there to get the experience for your application, and when you're ready, you have the money to get to Paris. Your plan isn't changed, just delayed a few months."

Val picked at her fingernails until she realized she was getting bits of nail polish on the dark carpet in his car. She did not know what to say. Her heart pounded. She would have more than enough money to travel to Paris and, in a few short months, a dream job in Boston. And with her experience at the MFA, *L'Académie de l'Art Magnifique* would be a sure thing. Her thoughts raced and she struggled to pull them together. Nathaniel was still awaiting a reply. "And what do you expect from me?"

One side of his mouth lifted in a smile—whether because he was impressed by her question or he'd won the battle, she didn't know.

Chapter Three

The next morning, Nathaniel pulled into the parking lot Val's apartment complex shared with a 24-hour convenience store, and he shut off his car. Many of the other buildings on the street had boarded-up windows and realtor signs. A dog barked from a second-story window and trash blew in the street. The atmosphere seemed ominous, even in the bright summer morning. He hoped Val was packed since he wasn't excited about leaving his car unattended for long in this neighborhood.

He thought back to the phone conversation he'd had with his friend Jason the previous day. Val wouldn't agree to anything until he'd secured a promise the MFA job was hers. He had to hand it to her, Valdosta McKinley knew how to negotiate.

He and Jason had shot the breeze about sports and caseloads until the conversation had a break and he knew his friend was wondering about the reason for his call. "I actually called to speak with Lisa."

Jason paused for an instant.

Nathaniel could almost see his friend's confused expression.

"Of course. She's right here." The sound of muffled voices came through the line as Jason gave the phone to his wife.

"Hi, Nathaniel. How are you doing?"

He heard the sympathy in her voice and realized they'd not talked since Clara's funeral. "Very well, thank you."

"Kids okay?"

"Yeah, they're doing really well. I've got them up here in Maine for the summer."

"Oh, that sounds wonderful. I wouldn't mind a vacation myself. How's that going?"

He thought she'd put a bit too much excitement into her voice. Maybe the extra enthusiasm about his vacation was intended as a nudge for her husband. "Good. Listen, Lisa, I called because I need a favor."

"Oh."

He heard a note of apprehension in her voice and didn't blame her for wondering what he would ask. While he and Jason had maintained a friendship over the years, the relationship had been mostly through professional contacts. He didn't know Lisa well and thought she must be feeling extremely awkward. But he plunged ahead anyway. "I need a nanny." He could almost feel her cringe over the phone line.

"Oh, Nathaniel, you know, I'm not really…"

"No, I've found someone, but the arrangement's a little complicated." He thought he heard Lisa exhale in relief and smiled. Getting someone to assume the worst case scenario was always a good strategy. After that, the real circumstance wouldn't seem so bad. "Her name's Valdosta McKinley. She was up here to work at a gallery in town—The Venus Gallery, I'm sure you've heard of it—anyway, I convinced her instead to work for me. She's got an Art History degree and is applying for a foreign internship, but she needs some experience working in her field after the summer's over." He knew he was misrepresenting the facts—but only slightly.

"And you told her you could get her a position at the MFA?"

Lisa didn't sound impressed, but Nathaniel kept at it. Persuading people to see things in a different light was what he did best. And if that didn't work, he had another ace up his sleeve. "I think she'll do a really good job. Like I said, she's got a degree."

"From where?"

This was the question he'd hoped she wouldn't ask, because he didn't have a way to sugarcoat his answer. "A college near her hometown in West Virginia." He grimaced as he said it, wishing there was a way to make Val's credentials sound more credible.

"Is this a joke?"

The coolness in her tone took him by surprise. Lisa wouldn't be as easy to convince as he'd thought. "Her degree might not be from the most prestigious school, but she's very charming and personable and—" he cleared his voice "—the kids and I are having a rough time. I need some help." He was disgusted he was using the "poor single dad" approach, but he needed this to happen.

The line was silent for a moment. "I really don't know if she'd work out, Nathaniel. I mean, I want to help you and the kids and everything, but…" She left the word hanging in the air.

Time to pull out the big guns. "I heard what you said about getting away. St. Thomas is beautiful this time of year, and my parents' condo is just sitting there on the beach, empty."

She chuckled. "Wow, you're good."

The details—Val's starting date and the condo

reservation—were settled in the next fifteen minutes.

When Nathaniel had texted Val to tell her the deal was in place, he hadn't received a response for hours. He assumed she'd slept after her accident. Later that evening, they'd made plans for him to pick her up first thing this morning.

He walked into the building, up the stairs, and down the dim hallway, locating the brass number 3 on the door and raised his hand to knock.

Val pulled open the door. "I saw you from the window." She jerked her thumb over her shoulder toward the room behind her. "You're right on time." She opened the door farther and dragged out an orange hard-sided suitcase.

Her luggage was apparently a survivor of the cold war. Nathaniel's quick glimpse of the space showed a metal-railed bed, a round table with two chairs, a microwave, hot plate, and small fridge. The apartment looked like a drug dealer's crash pad on a crime drama. He wondered if she were ashamed he'd seen the conditions she was living in. "How are you feeling?" He hoped to give her something neutral to talk about to alleviate any discomfort she might be feeling.

"Much better. Thanks to pain medicine, a long nap, and of course my nutritious meal." Val tossed her ponytail to the side as she slung the furry purse over her shoulder. "You can just pull the door shut. It locks on its own, and I left the key inside for the landlord." She waited for Nathaniel to shut the door. "Hall could use some light, but it's a nice place, don't ya think?"

She acted confident and cheerful, and didn't seem embarrassed by her circumstance at all. "Is this everything?" Nathaniel waved his hand toward her suitcase.

"I travel light." She lifted her shoulders and grinned.

Her smile brightened the gloomy hallway. Nathaniel was surprised by the change in her appearance from the day before. Without all the makeup, her face looked fresh and healthy. Her hair was pulled back, and instead of enormous, stiff curls, gentle waves hung from her ponytail. Her outfit was another story. Cut-off jean shorts that showed way too much of her legs, and a bright green tank top with a silk-screened silhouette of cowboy boots. He could only imagine what Lisa would say when Val arrived to give tours at the MFA. He reached to take the suitcase.

Val held onto the handle. "I'm your employee now, Mr. Cavanaugh. You shouldn't be carrying my luggage."

"My mother raised me to be a gentleman." He gave a small bow, sweeping his hand to the side.

"Why, you sure do know just what to say to a southern girl." Her smile grew, exposing dimples in her cheeks. She set down the suitcase, pressed the back of her hand to her forehead, and batted her eyes.

He wondered how much time had passed since he'd joked like this with someone. How had he missed those dimples the day before? Val was turning out to be nothing like he would have imagined. When Nathaniel lifted her suitcase, he was surprised by how little it weighed. This one bag contained all her clothes, everything she'd brought with her to work in Maine and then to move to Paris? His late wife had packed more for a weekend getaway. Thoughts of Clara cast a pall over his mood, as they always did. He turned and led the way silently outside to his car.

Luckily, the vehicle was untouched. He loaded the suitcase into the trunk, noticing large cracks in the sides had been duct taped. He hoped she'd purchase better luggage for her international flight. He walked to where Val waited next to the passenger door. The sunlight revealed dark scrapes surrounded by crimson splotches on Val's leg and elbow. He cringed inside at the sight. The need to keep her clothing from rubbing against her injuries was probably behind her choice of outfit. Nathaniel unlocked and opened the door.

Val looked up at the shabby brick building. One side of her mouth lifted in a thoughtful smile. "Funny how something like this would make me sentimental after just a few days." She stepped behind the car door and pointed up at the window. "This was my first apartment. The first time I didn't have to share a bed with my little sisters." She smiled and shrugged. "Well, on to a new adventure, right?"

Nathaniel considered her words as he walked around the front of the car. The apartment was small and dilapidated, set in a neighborhood where he'd be nervous to walk after dark, and yet she was sad to leave it behind. What did that say about where she'd come from? He truly had no idea what this woman's life had been like. From small hints she'd given, her childhood could not have been any more different from his own upbringing if she'd been raised on Mars. He slid behind the steering wheel and turned the key.

"Ya didn't bring Ruby and Finn?" Val asked.

He shook his head. He hadn't known how long loading her things would take, and hadn't wanted to bring his children into this neighborhood where he didn't know how well he could keep an eye on them. Not after yesterday. "Mrs. Spencer, the housekeeper, agreed to watch them this morning."

"Y'all have a housekeeper, and you need a nanny, too?"

"Mrs. Spencer cleans the house once a week, and she stops by every other day to deliver groceries and cook some meals."

She nodded once and sat up in her seat. "But now you won't need her anymore."

"And why is that?"

Val snapped her head around and stared with squinted eyes. "Surely for the amount of money y'all are paying me, you don't expect me to have someone else do my cooking and cleaning. I'm perfectly capable of keeping up a house and feeding a family."

"No. I don't intend for you to do any of that. Your sole responsibility is Ruby and Finn." Surprise jerked his head backward and he gave her a sideways glance. He thought most women would have preferred to have a housekeeper instead of volunteering to perform the tasks themselves.

"I imagine they'd help me. Ruby is old enough to sweep a floor, and even Finn could use a dust rag."

Nathaniel glanced at her as he turned onto the main road. He shook his head. "They'll be plenty busy with their summer studies. And of course, productive play time."

"Summer studies?" Val folded her arms and tipped her head to the side. "Ruby and Finn? They're so young."

Nathaniel fixed his gaze on the road, tapping his fingers on the steering wheel. "I take it you're not

41

familiar with early development coursework." Perhaps she thought his children should attend public school and end up in a community college in the middle of nowhere. Val was a poster child for the foolishness of that academic pathway. The preparatory academy Ruby attended and Finn would start in a year was one of, if not the actual, best in the country. And competing at that level required a substantial amount of home study during the summer, as well as tutors during the school year.

"I mean, I'm not telling you how to raise your kids." Val twisted to face him. "But I think there's got to be a balance, don't you? Playtime, learning, and work. Course you want their minds stimulated and for them to feel important and loved, but a satisfaction comes from having responsibility and working hard…"

Nathaniel's face was set, and he suspected that was why Val had stopped speaking. He'd not anticipated she'd challenge his parenting style. Not that the opinion of a redneck woman who dressed like a hillbilly contestant on a reality show, and whose child rearing experience came from looking after her brothers and sisters in a trailer, carried much weight.

"But they're your children, and you're my boss. I was just giving my opinion. I'm sorry if y'all were offended." Val turned back to face the windshield.

Her voice was softer, but she didn't sound remorseful in the least. He tightened his fingers on the wheel and counted to ten in his head.

They rode in silence. Nathaniel drove through the outskirts of Lobster Cove, past grand colorful houses with stained glass and window boxes. The streets were picturesque with well-tended gardens and charming old-fashioned looking street lights. Leaving the residential area behind, the road followed the rocky shoreline along the cliffs. Below them, elegant windjammers, sturdy lobster boats, and tourist ferries shared the harbor.

He turned the car onto a gravel road lined with trees that nearly touched above them, sending dappled shadows over the ground, and he glanced at Val, wondering what her thoughts were as she watched the scenery through the window. Nathaniel had thought his oldest friend Seth was crazy for moving all the way out here a few years ago, but the moment Nathaniel arrived for a visit, he'd fallen in love with this town and the friendly, quirky residents, and their casual lifestyle. He'd hoped his kids would feel the comfort of Lobster Cove, too, and they'd enjoy themselves, moving at a slower pace than their busy city lives required.

"Seth's house is down that way." He pointed to the side of the road as they passed a turn off. "He's our closest neighbor."

Val turned her head.

He knew she wouldn't see Seth's house through the thick trees. "Our place is at the end of the road." He wondered why he felt the need to fill the silence.

They emerged into a clearing where Val would get her first view of the cottage. He watched from the corner of his eye to see her reaction.

Val's eyes widened. She touched her fingers to her lips. "Oh my." Her voice was slightly above a whisper.

He smiled to himself. When he'd seen the cottage for the first time, he'd had a similar reaction. The Victorian-style house was two stories with a pointed gabled roof. The wood was painted blue-gray with

43

white trim and shutters. Flowering bushes bordered the walkway and a large porch wrapped around the entire house. The cottage sat on a point, jutting out into the Atlantic, with magnificent ocean views in all directions. Couthy Cottage looked like a postcard.

"It's so beautiful." Val breathed out a sigh. She opened the car door and stepped out.

Nathaniel walked around the car to join her and allowed his muscles to relax. He hadn't realized how anxious he'd been for her approval, and the expression on her face left no doubt that she was awestruck. For a moment, he enjoyed the feeling of impressing her. Heaven knew he'd never managed to do it with Clara. His late wife would have hated everything about this place. No shopping, no room service.

The cottage door opened, and Ruby ran down the stairs, throwing her arms around Val's waist.

Val flinched.

Nathaniel put his hand on Ruby's shoulder. "Be gentle, Ruby. Remember Val's still hurting from yesterday." The grateful look his new nanny gave him made his heart trip ever so slightly. He must still be relishing her delight at seeing the cottage.

"Come inside." Ruby pulled Val toward the house. "Come see your bedroom. It's right by mine."

Mrs. Spencer stepped onto the porch with Finn. She was a tall, thin woman who wore her hair pulled back into a tight bun.

Nathaniel introduced the women.

"How do ya do, ma'am?" Val held out her hand.

The housekeeper's gaze traveled over Val's ensemble as the women shook hands. Her brow rose a tick, but she refrained from comment.

Finn held up his arms, and Val lifted the boy onto her hip. She pointed to a brass plaque next to the front door. "Couthy Cottage?"

"A lot of the old houses around here have Scottish names," Nathaniel said. "The owner told me Couthy means cozy—or pleasant. Seth's is called Hyne House. I think it means something like haven."

Val followed Ruby through the house.

"This is where we watch movies, and we eat in the kitchen. Daddy's room is down the hall by his office, and our bedrooms are upstairs," Ruby chattered as she pulled Val from room to room.

His daughter seemed more excited than he'd seen her about anything for months. Nathaniel waited in the entryway until Val and the children came back down the stairs. "I hope the accommodations are acceptable?" He pushed his hands into his pockets and rocked back on his heels.

Val's gaze traveled around the space and when he spoke, she blinked. "Sir? Oh, sorry, I...yes, everything is wonderful. Couthy Cottage, it's..." Her gaze met his.

Her soft smile tugged at his heart again.

"I love it." She came of her haze and straightened her shoulders. "Mr. Cavanaugh, you said something about lessons?"

"I already did my lessons for today." Ruby still held onto Val's hand. "I want to play outside."

Nathaniel nodded in response to Val's questioning expression. "I'll show you their workbooks tomorrow."

She turned to the kids and held out her arms, grinning. "All right, Miss Ruby, Captain Finn. Y'all lead the way." She left with the children through the back door, promising to return at lunch time.

Nathaniel walked down the hallway to his office and sat back in the chair behind the desk, opening his laptop and feeling at once relieved that he could get some work done undisturbed, and a little guilty that he had so readily given over his children to the care of a stranger. The worry that he wasn't feeling more nervous grew, and he finally pushed back from his desk.

He walked through the kitchen and out on the back porch, leaning against the wooden railing as he watched Val, Ruby, and Finn walk carefully down the path to the beach. The small cove beneath the cottage was secluded, but the beach wasn't a sandy, no-shoes area. Rocks and shells, seaweed, as well as driftwood and other flotsam the waves saw fit to dislodge covered the shore.

Further around the cove were tide pools that he hoped to take the children to explore but still hadn't gotten around to with all the work piling up.

Ruby handed Val what Nathaniel assumed was a seashell, and the three of them took turns holding it, talking about it, lifting it up to study at different angles.

Eventually, Val put it into her pocket. The treasure was quickly joined by another she made an equally grand production over.

Finn handed an object to Val and while she turned it over in her hands, Ruby screamed.

Nathaniel's heart flew into his throat as he clenched his muscles, ready to bolt toward the beach.

Val ran to Ruby.

Ruby continued to scream.

Val followed the girl's pointing finger. She hurried in the direction she indicated and picked up a crab that was large enough Nathaniel could see it from the house. She glanced at it and tossed it into the sea with a flick of her wrist.

He knew from firsthand experience that those black crabs could be nasty. It had probably been running toward Ruby, its claws opening and closing, making a clicking sound that most likely terrified his daughter. Val hadn't hesitated for an instant. His confidence in the suitability of his nanny rose another notch.

As they explored, Val stopped and pulled on what looked to Nathaniel like some driftwood. With some effort, she dislodged what turned out to be a battered rowboat that was missing half of its boards, and set it upright. She helped the children climb inside and their laughter carried toward him over the swish of the waves as they played in the boat.

Nathaniel was amazed Val didn't seem worried about dirtying her clothes or getting splinters. She somehow managed to be a playmate, as well as someone his children—and he, for that matter—could trust. His phone buzzed, and he realized he'd been watching Val and his children play for nearly an hour. They would come in for lunch soon, and he hadn't gotten any work done. In spite of his lack of professional productivity this morning, he was at ease, his body feeling light as he walked back to his office, reassured that hiring Val had been the right move for his family.

****

That evening, Val pulled up the blankets around Finn's shoulders, pushing his still-damp and shampoo-smelling hair off his forehead. He was asleep before she even turned off the light.

"Ruby, did you get on your jammies?" Val walked into the room next to Finn's. She picked up the damp towel from the floor and laid it over the back of a chair.

Ruby sat in her bed wearing a blue silky nightgown. "My mother used to read me a book before bed."

Val would have gone crazy for that nightgown when she was a six-year old girl. "Do you want me to read to you?"

"No." Ruby spoke quickly and then raised her gaze to Val's, her lip quivering. "I'm sorry."

"Don't be sorry." Seeing the sadness in the little girl's eyes made her heart ache. She knew all too well the hurt of losing a mother. "Reading a bedtime story was something special between you and your momma. It's okay that you don't want to share it with someone else."

Ruby was quiet. She bit her lip and twisted a ribbon from her nightgown around her finger.

"Do ya wanna know what *my* momma did at bedtime?" Val sat at the foot of Ruby's bed and scooted back to lean against the wall. "She would pretend to put me under a sleeping spell. She waved her fingers above my toes, and tell me my toes were asleep, then my feet and legs. Once part of me was under the spell, the rule was, I couldn't move it. My eyes were the very last thing. She kissed me good night and waved her fingers over my eyes, and I closed them and fell asleep."

Ruby pulled at the stitching on her bedspread. "Sometimes, I'm worried I'll forget my mother. I have a picture of her, but I don't remember what her voice sounded like."

Val watched her for a moment before she made up

her mind. "I'm going to show you something that I never showed anyone, not even my sisters." She slid off the bed, careful not to rub her sore leg along the bedspread, and then hurried to her room. When she returned, she sat cross-legged on the bed, facing Ruby. "This is a book I made after my momma died. I was afraid, just like you, that I would forget things about her, so…well, let me show you."

Val opened the book between them and turned it around to face Ruby. "This here's a picture of me and my momma when I was a baby. She was pretty, don't ya think?" She turned the page.

Ruby leaned forward.

"A napkin I found in her purse. See here, is a smear of her lipstick. I kept it so I could remember what color she wore. And this is a picture I cut out of a magazine. I stuck it in here to remember that we saw this movie at the drive-in. A gum wrapper. She loved mint gum, but not peppermint." Val continued explaining to Ruby about the things she'd taped in the book. "When I remember something, I write it down." She ran her finger over a lined page covered in handwritten words. "These are the lyrics to a song momma used to sing."

Ruby studied the book, turning the pages gently.

The way she pinched her brows together and pursed her lips made her look more like a small adult than a young girl. As she watched Ruby, Val pulled her knees to her chest. "If you want, maybe we could buy ya a book in town, and I'd help you write down things about your momma. Things like her reading you a story at night. Then you won't forget. What do ya think?" She hoped she wouldn't upset Ruby's father by offering such a personal activity.

"Can we do it tomorrow?" Ruby looked up and her eyes widened.

The sight of her hopeful expression melted Val's heart. "I'll ask your daddy."

She turned her gaze down to the book and ran her fingers over a page. "Daddy doesn't like to talk about Mother."

"Maybe it makes him too sad." Val brushed her fingers over Ruby's arm. "Or maybe he thinks it will make you sad." She took the small hand in her own. "I have a brother, Manly, who never wants to talk about Momma, ever. He doesn't even like it when one of us talks about her. But his attitude doesn't mean he didn't love her. It's just his way of keeping her memory special. Just like this book is *my* way."

Ruby furrowed her brows.

"Now you better go to sleep, or you'll be too tired to have any fun tomorrow." Val moved the book off Ruby's bed and tucked the blankets over her body.

"Will you put a sleeping spell on me, Val?"

"Of course I will." Val's eyes blurred and her throat tightened as she wiggled her fingers above Ruby, putting parts of her body to sleep. The memory of her mother combined with the love she was starting to feel for this child filled her chest with a warmth that she wasn't prepared for. She kissed Ruby on the forehead and wiggled her fingers in front of her face.

Ruby closed her eyes.

"Sleep tight, Miss Ruby," Val whispered and closed the door behind her.

Val's phone beeped, and she checked her messages. Just Seth making sure she took the pain medication he'd sent over and reminding her to apply some anti-bacterial ointment before she went to sleep. She smiled at the thoughtful gesture, even though she was feeling a bit smothered by all the attention. *Hadn't any of these people ever had road rash?*

She called home, checking on her daddy and sisters, and then left the memory book in her room before walking downstairs and out to the back balcony. All day she'd been hoping to sit in the quiet and listen to the waves. Even though the time was well past 8:30, the sun was just dipping below the horizon and the sky was still bright. She rested her forearms on the railing. The view was amazing. The blues and grays in the water carried golden shimmers of light, and Val wondered how she would capture the effect with paint. The cottage was surrounded on three sides by water, and the other by forest. Val felt as if they were in their own world. Isolated, and yet exposed at the same time. "It's magical," she said softly into the wind.

The sound of Nathaniel clearing his throat startled her and she gasped, spinning and banging her bruised hip into the railing. She spread her fingers over her collarbone, trying to recapture her breath.

He sat in on one of the wooden chairs behind her, his hand around a bottle of Lighthouse Lager on the armrest. "Sorry. I didn't mean to surprise you. Just thought I should warn you that you're not alone."

"No harm done." Val placed both palms on the railing and leaned her lower back against it. "Am I invading your privacy?"

"Hardly." He spread his hand toward the chair next to his. "Can I get ya a drink?"

"Y'all got a jigger of moonshine?" She crossed the space and eased into the chair. The Adirondack style hadn't appeared particularly comfortable, but once she sat and leaned back against the smooth wood, she changed her mind.

His mouth pulled in a half-smile. "Just beer."

Val hadn't seen an unguarded smile from Nathaniel, and the sight surprised her. Maybe the alcohol was responsible for loosening him up, or maybe he was more relaxed in the evening after the kids were safely in bed. The expression was a welcome change from the buttoned-up serious lawyer she'd known for the last two days. "I'm only teasing. I don't drink at work."

He rested his head against the back of the chair and studied her through half-lidded eyes. "How was your first day with the kids?"

"Honestly, this job is a dream."

"That's a description I don't hear too often from my employees."

"I've never been to a place like this. And let's face it, if it weren't for y'all, I probably never would. It's beautiful, the kids are perfect, and I'm being paid to spend the summer in the most wonderful house I've ever seen." She shifted on the low chair, pulling her knee to her chest and resting her foot on the seat so her raw skin didn't stick to the painted wood. "My room, the ocean…everything. I can't thank you enough for this arrangement, Mr. Cavanaugh. I should have told you earlier."

"I love this cottage, too. The first time I saw it, I couldn't wait to bring my family up here." He turned his head to look out over the water.

"I still can't believe y'all call this a cottage. In Millford Creek, it would be considered a mansion. My friend, Twyla Fay, lives in a house that used to be a motel. Every room opens to the outside. I always thought how fancy her place was, but *this*..." She swept her hand around to include the house and the view and sighed.

"I know exactly what you mean." He turned to her and a small smile played over his mouth. "Except that part about Twyla Fay, and how in the world do you convert a motel into a house?" He closed his eyes as he rested his head back again. "But you're right. This place is special."

Chapter Four

Nathaniel allowed the sound of the waves crashing into the rocky shoreline to lull him into a blissful stupor, assisted in part by the alcohol. He planned to spend every evening precisely in this spot, with the cool sea breeze blowing, a local brew in his hand, and his phone's power turned off.

"Mr. Cavanaugh?"

He opened his eyes, remembering that Val still sat next to him. The setting sun put golden highlights in her hair and sparkles in her eyes. He thought maybe he should re-think his evening beverage consumption if his nanny made his heartbeat speed up.

Val picked at her nail polish. "I hope I didn't overstep my bounds, but Ruby talked to me a bit about her momma. I told her I'd help her make a scrap book to record some of her memories." Her gaze moved to his. "I hoped that would be all right with you."

Nathaniel didn't answer. The truth was, he'd overheard the entire conversation between Ruby and Val, and that was part of the reason he was on his fourth beer. Val had made him sound like a hero, or a tortured widower, when the truth was, Nathaniel was neither. The familiar ache of guilt wrenched his stomach, and he took a deep drink in hopes of dulling it.

I'm sorry, sir. I didn't mean to make you...I'm

sorry." Val reached toward him but drew back her hand. She stood, wincing when she shifted her weight.

Still, he said nothing. What was there to say? Would he spill his deepest secrets to this person he'd met yesterday? Tell her the truth about his marriage? Tell her she had no reason to worry about his feelings because he wasn't a devastated husband?

Val shifted from foot to foot and scratched her arm. A few awkward moments later, she spoke. "I'm truly sorry. I...Good night, Mr. Cavanaugh." She turned and hurried into the house.

Nathaniel continued to stew over the thoughts he'd mulled over for months. What if he had brought home the divorce papers a day earlier? Or later? Would everything be different? Would Clara still be alive? As it turned out, he'd ended up with the pity of everyone he met, looking like a poor, heartbroken man when he was actually the reason his wife was dead.

He took his guilt out on those around him, pulling away from family and friends, and now he'd offended this woman whose only crime was helping his daughter. Even though she was gone, Clara still managed to make him feel like nothing he did was ever good enough.

When he met Seth for their run the next morning, he was still dwelling on the way he'd acted toward Val. If he hadn't known his friend would be waiting where the road branched, Nathaniel would have slept in and nursed his headache.

"Morning, Daisy." Nathaniel scratched Seth's golden retriever behind her ears.

"Late night?" Seth asked as they set a pace through the forest.

Daisy bounded along next to them.

"Do I look it?"

"Red eyes, pale…I'd guess you either had a few too many, or your new nanny has already brought you to tears.

"The former. And I might have brought *her* to tears."

"Val?" Seth whipped around his head. "What happened?"

Nathaniel didn't sense any disapproval in Seth's tone, but knowing his friend, that didn't necessarily mean he felt as casual as he sounded. Seth was likely one of the least judgmental people he knew, which was one reason Nathaniel found confiding in him to be so easy. But based on his reaction, Seth also had a soft spot for Val. "She asked me if it would be all right to help Ruby with a scrapbook of memories about her mother."

"And…" Seth prompted, raising his hand.

Nathaniel shrugged. He lifted the hem of his T-shirt to wipe sweat from his forehead.

"You didn't know how to handle it and so, you…"

"Didn't."

Seth skirted around a dip in the road and rejoined him. "And Val thought you were hurt, or angry with her action."

"Val's managed to connect with my daughter in two days better than I have in six years. I should be down on my knees thanking her for getting Ruby to open up about her feelings. Instead, I…"

They ran several yards in silence before Seth spoke.

"Val's a big girl. From what you've told me, she's known loss herself. She doesn't seem like the type to hold a grudge."

"So, you don't think I need to…"

Seth nodded once. "You definitely need to."

They turned onto the main road, running along the tops of the sea cliffs until they reached a path that led down to a long, flat stretch of beach.

Nathaniel knew Seth was right. He owed Val an apology. The entire conversation was making him uncomfortable, and he redirected it back on his friend. "You seem to understand her pretty well. Are you going to start dating my nanny?" He tried to keep his voice light, but he definitely didn't like the idea. His friend having a relationship with his employee was unprofessional, and he…he just didn't like it.

"Nope. Val's not my type." Seth picked up a branch and threw it down the beach. He increased his pace as he ran over the rocky shore.

Daisy ran through the surf to retrieve it.

Nathaniel felt a confusing mix of relief and disbelief. He nearly stumbled over a piece of driftwood. "What do you mean she's not your type?" He matched his pace to Seth's. Was she too friendly? Too beautiful? Too happy? Too easy to talk with? What was wrong with Seth, and why was Nathaniel suddenly so defensive?

"I'm a caretaker. Val won't let anyone baby her. She's too independent for me."

Nathaniel was surprised by his friend's honesty. Since the men had reconnected, Seth listened to him spill his guts about everything about his wife's death, his feelings of inadequacy when it came to rearing his children, and stress about the direction his career was taking him. The morning runs became more of a therapy session for Nathaniel, and this was the first time Seth spoke about himself so personally.

They reached the end of the flat beach and took another trail.

"So, what do you have to say for your Red Sox after last night's game?" Seth glanced back to make sure the dog followed, and the men switched into an easy dialog on neutral topics as they re-entered the shade of the forest and ran back up the gravel road.

When they reached the turnoff to Seth's house, they used the rails of an old fence to lean against as they stretched out.

"I may have to go back to Boston for a few days next week." Nathaniel pulled his arm across his chest. "Mind checking in on Val and the kids?"

"Sure." Seth held on to a rail and reached back to grab his ankle as he stretched his quad. "And you're going to…"

"I'll talk to her today."

****

When Nathaniel returned to the house, he found Val and the children in the kitchen. Ruby and Finn worked in their notebooks at the table while Val wiped down the counter.

When he saw his father, Finn jumped up and ran to him.

Ruby waved her fingers in front of her nose at Nathaniel's sweaty smell.

Val glanced up when he entered and turned to rinse her cloth under the tap.

Nathaniel complimented Ruby on the words she was writing, told Finn to keep up the good work on coloring shapes, and walked to the sink.

"Mornin' Mr. Cavanaugh. Me and the kids had yogurt and toast for breakfast. Can I get you—"

"Val, can I talk to you for a moment?"

Her gaze darted to his, and she blinked quickly. She dried off her hands on a dishtowel, glanced once at the children who were bent over their books, and then followed him out to the porch.

Nathaniel hadn't realized he'd upset her so badly the night before until he saw the worry in her expression. He closed the door behind her and turned to where she stood, her arms folded as she chewed on her thumbnail. "I need to apologize for the way I behaved last night."

Val's breath hitched.

"A memory book sounds like the perfect way for Ruby to heal. Thank you for thinking of it, and offering to help her."

"I thought you were fixin' to fire me." Val's eyes were wet, and she spoke in a soft voice. "I was worried all night."

Nathaniel wanted to kick himself for what he'd put her through. "I'm sorry for upsetting you. On the subject of emotions, I…have a difficult time, and then on top of it, I had a little alcohol in me. I should not have treated you that way."

She uncrossed her arms and started picking at her nail polish. "I know what it's like to lose someone. We all handle it differently."

"Some of us don't handle it at all." He shoved his hands into his pockets. Val's gaze met his straight-on, and a sense of relief washed over him. The idea of her being upset because of him had bothered him more than he'd realized. He held out his hand. "Still friends?"

Val took his hand and shook. "Course. Now, get yourself showered, and I'll fry up some eggs for y'all before the kids and I head into town for story time at the Shuckers Booktique."

He held open the screen door and when she passed and thanked him, he saw the dimpled smile he'd hoped for.

****

Saturday came quicker than Val would have believed possible. Being a nanny for the Cavanaugh family was a dream job. Every day she looked forward to spending time with the kids and seeing Nathaniel on the porch in the evenings. She loved the routine they'd fallen into, and with some reluctance, she put on her swimsuit under her clothes, took a towel and a book, and headed out past the Sea Crest Inn to spend her day off lying out on the only sandy beach in town.

Spreading her towel, she thought of how Ruby and Finn would love to play in the fine sand. She'd have to bring them next week. One of the shops in town sold buckets and sand shovels, and Val thought maybe she would pick up a couple on her way home. She watched the boats in the harbor for a while, then lay back to read, but she was lulled to sleep by the call of seagulls, the shouts of watermen, the clang of bells, and beneath it all, the ever- present swishing of waves as they ebbed and flowed from the shore.

A voice startled her, and she blinked herself awake, shading her face with her hand as she sat up.

The man that had spoken shifted to the side to block the sun. "Sorry to wake yah. I asked if this spot is taken." He waved his hand toward the sand next to her towel.

She felt uncomfortably vulnerable with a strange man standing over her, but his face seemed friendly. "No. It's all yours."

He smiled, dropped a grocery bag on the sand, and spread out a towel. He took off his T-shirt, flopping down on his stomach next to her. "I'm Brandt." He fished around in the bag. "Chips?"

"Thanks." She took a handful of potato chips from his offered bag. "Val."

"You look like yah been chewed up and spit out, Val." He lifted his chin to indicate her injuries. "How'd a pretty gahl get such bad scrapes? And your bruise..." He made a tsking sound as he shook his head. "Pity."

Brandt's hair was the color of caramel, and his skin deeply tanned. When he shifted position, the muscles on his arms bulged. "Trolley accident," Val said. She'd never heard an accent quite like Brandt's, and wanted to hear him speak again. When he said her name, he pronounced it Vahl.

He lifted his brows and nodded his head, "Heard about that. Saved a kid, didn't yah?"

Val shrugged, eating another chip. She didn't want to talk about the accident or the Cavanaughs with this stranger. She shifted onto her stomach, leaning forward on her elbows and turned her face toward him. "Where are you from? I've never heard anyone talk like you."

Brandt laughed. "Then you haven't been in Maine long. I'm a local boy. And as far as accents go, yours is the cutest I've ever heard. You a southern gahl?"

"I'm from West Virginia."

"I could listen to you talk all day, Val." He lifted his gaze to look past her and waved.

Val turned her head and saw a group approaching

with towels and coolers. They all appeared to be roughly the same age as she and Brandt.

"Yah mind if some of my friends join us?"

"Course not."

Brandt introduced Val as the "gahl who got hit by the trolley." His friends immediately welcomed her into their group. They unloaded drinks and snacks. A few of them threw a football, and Val found herself chatting with some of the other women.

"What do you do here in Lobster Cove?" A woman named Alice handed her a bag of licorice.

"I'm working as a nanny for Mr. Cavanaugh. He's staying with his kids at a vacation cottage outside of town."

"Not bad." Alice turned down the corners of her mouth and raised her brows as she nodded.

Val listened to the local gossip, chatted about movies, and told a bit about her home town. She found that some of the group was working in Lobster Cove for the summer and others were locals like Brandt. They were accepting and friendly, and the day flew by.

Before she knew it, Val's skin was starting to feel burned. She pulled her phone out of her bag and saw the hour was already late afternoon. She stood and pulled her T-shirt back on. "I had a great day with y'all, but I should be getting back."

Brandt picked up her towel and shook off the sand then handed it to her. "Some of the guys are having a clambake tonight down on Craigwood Beach. You wanna be my date?"

Val thought about Ruby and Finn...and Nathaniel. Would they be missing her? Did Finn get a good nap today? Did Ruby get a chance to work on her memory book? She wanted to be home with the kids and put them to bed, and then visit with Nathaniel on the porch as the sun set. She'd almost made up her mind to say no to Brandt, until something in the back of her mind stopped her. She was acting as if the Cavanaughs were her family, but in truth, *they* were the family, and she was an outsider who would leave in a few months and never see them again. The more she allowed herself to get swallowed up in the fairy tale of belonging in the Couthy Cottage, of being part of their family, the harder leaving them in August would be.

She looked around at her new friends. She liked the idea of having a group to hang out with on her day off, and for her own sake, she needed to have a bit of distance. A relationship with people other than the Cavanaughs would lessen the sting of saying goodbye. "I'll check and let ya know in an hour. Would that work?" she asked Brandt. Her day off probably extended into the evening, but the details hadn't ever been discussed.

"Sure." He typed his number into her phone and handed it back. "I hope you can make it."

Val said her good-byes and slipped on her flip flops. She walked across the sand, up the patio steps, and out to the parking lot where she'd left the car she was using for the summer. She drove through the town and up the cliff road, wishing the drive didn't feel like she was going...*home*.

****

Brandt had wanted to pick her up at eight, but Val asked if they could push it back in order to give her time to tuck in the kids. She'd barely finished putting a sleeping spell on Ruby when she heard an engine outside. After ducking into her room, she grabbed her jacket and hurried down the stairs.

Nathaniel was walking through the entryway toward his office.

"Mr. Cavanaugh." Val called out; although after she did, she wondered what had made her catch his attention. The hour would be late when she returned, and she had become accustomed to Nathaniel being the last person she spoke to before she went to sleep.

He turned and his gaze traveled quickly over her sundress and then rested on her face. "Yes?"

For the most fleeting second, she wondered whether he thought she looked cute in the dress. She loved the look of the spaghetti straps and sweetheart neckline. "I just…Good night."

"Wear your jacket." He motioned toward the hoodie she'd slung over her arm. "The beach gets cool at night." He walked to his office.

"Thanks." The fleeting image of Nathaniel sitting on the porch alone while the sun set floated through her mind. She opened the door, chiding herself. *He's probably delighted at the chance to have an evening to himself.*

Brandt waved as she approached his motorcycle. He handed her a helmet which would only make her messy bun that much messier. She zipped up her jacket, crammed the helmet on her head, and climbed on behind him, wishing she'd worn something else. The sundress looked cute, the fabric didn't irritate her scraped leg, but a motorcycle ride in a short skirt…she hoped Craigwood Beach wasn't too far.

After about fifteen minutes of bumpy road and cold wind, Brandt pulled off the main road and parked next to a group of cars. They made their way down the gravel path through the trees to the beach. Brandt put his arm around her, his fingers playing over the skin on her shoulder.

She wasn't completely comfortable with his familiarity, but so far, his intentions seemed friendly enough. Val decided if he got much more handsy, she'd put him in his place.

The beach wasn't sandy like the one by the Sea Crest Inn. Between the pine trees, rocks and crushed shells covered the ground topped with bits of driftwood.

They found their group sitting on logs around a campfire with plates of food and open coolers.

Val greeted her new friends.

"Yah ever been to a clambake before?" Brandt handed her a plate.

She shook her head. "I've never even tasted a clam."

"Well, Miss McKinley, yer in for a treat." He led her away from the fire and showed her the pit dug into the sand where wet seaweed had steamed the clams, lobster, and other shellfish. They each filled a plate with potatoes, carrots, corn on the cob, and seafood and then returned to the campfire to join the others.

Val spread her jacket over the log to protect her legs when she sat. The beach seemed even darker because of the firelight, the trees rustled in the wind and the waves flowed, but she couldn't see the water.

"Now some are squeamish about seafood they have to crack out of their shells, but the fresher the better. There's nothing to worry about." Brandt used a plastic fork to open a clam and dig out the soft meat.

Val didn't think she had ever turned down food in

her life. She figured those who had didn't know what being hungry felt like. "It smells delicious." Val followed Brandt's lead and pried open a clam, popping the warm chewy meat into her mouth. The bite turned out to be better than she would have guessed, but the warm, juicy lobster tasted like heaven.

"I had no idea seafood could taste so good." She worked another chunk of lobster meat out of the shell. "I admit, my experience is with canned salmon and whatever my brothers caught in the stream by my house."

Brandt laughed and pulled a beer out of the cooler. He offered one to Val, but she declined.

Val listened to the conversation around the fire, joining in occasionally. The food was delicious, and she enjoyed the company, but her mind traveled back to the cottage more often than she would have liked. Was Nathaniel sitting on the porch alone this evening?

A younger woman with a dark ponytail joined their group, sitting on the log next to Val. She introduced herself as Candice, and she and Val exchanged pleasantries while Brandt passed around more bottles of beer. From her giggles, Candice had apparently already had a few.

Val passed again on the alcohol. The last thing she wanted to do was return to the cottage tipsy and smelling like booze. Not that she thought Nathaniel would mind. He wasn't her dad, after all, but she didn't want to give him any reason to question her competence about caring for his children. Candice was local, too, and Val thought the Maine accent sounded different on a woman. Harsher.

"Vahl, where are ya stayin in town?" Candice took

a deep swig of Lighthouse Lager.

"I'm working as a nanny up at Couthy Cottage. Do y'all know where that is?"

Candice dropped her mouth. "You're living with the handsome Boston lawyer in the vacation cottage by Dr. Goodwyn? How'd you swing that?" Her gaze dropped to the neckline of Val's low-cut dress. "Oh." She tipped her head and raised a brow. "I guess even rich guys like their women a little trashy."

"Like I said, I'm his nanny." Val tried to keep the anger and offense out of her voice.

"Ya." Candice winked theatrically. "His *nanny*."

Val was stunned. She kept her smile pleasant as she excused herself to get a drink of water. She slipped her arms into her jacket sleeves and zipped it up as she walked toward the ice bucket. Candice was obviously inebriated and catty, and Val couldn't care less what the woman thought of her. But the idea Nathaniel might think of her as trashy felt like a rock in her stomach. She did care what *he* thought of her. She'd rarely known anyone who had treated her so well. Especially one who led a life so much more affluent than hers.

A memory flooded her mind, despite her best efforts to quell it. She was sixteen and dating the captain of the basketball team, Bo Callaway. They attended the same high school, but Bo lived in the nearby town of Anabelle, in the wealthiest neighborhood in the county. His father owned the mine that employed Val's daddy. Bo talked to her on the phone every night, held her hands in the halls, and kissed her under the bleachers. He'd even had flowers delivered to the drugstore where she worked. Val was head over heels in love, and she was certain he felt the same.

After the biggest basketball game of the year against their rival team, the Wolverines, Val waited in the hallway outside the locker room to surprise Bo. She'd gotten the night off work and attended the game. He would undoubtedly be thrilled to see her.

The locker room door opened. The sound of high school basketball players, fresh off a victory, blasted like a wave into the darkened hall.

Val's breath caught as she heard Bo teasing with the guys on the team.

"I hope all y'all are planning to come out to my daddy's party at the country club." His voice carried over the laughter and excited sounds of the other players.

The boys cheered and the mood of excitement was joined by a sense of anticipation.

"You better believe I am."

"Wouldn't miss it."

"And you bringing Val?"

Her heart raced, and she stepped back into a doorway in the shadows of the hall, feeling shy and at the same time excited about the idea of hearing Bo talk about her. She strained her ears as her smile grew and her heart beat faster.

"Nah. Val's fun. But she's not the kind of girl you take home to momma. And ain't no way I'm breaking up with her until after high school. She's too hot." Bo's voice hung in Val's ears even after the team moved past the darkened doorway and headed to the parking lot.

Val's stomach was so heavy that she didn't think her legs would hold her. She slid down, leaning her back against the doorway. She could imagine the guys piling into their nice cars and trucks and meeting their girlfriends at the country club. Those girls—the ones who dressed in cute new clothes, lived in a house in the suburbs, and had their hair and nails done at a real beauty parlor—they were the kind Bo wouldn't be ashamed to take home to his momma. The weight in Val's stomach turned to shame, and her face burned. Why had she thought Bo considered her as any kind of an equal? She lived in a trailer in the holler, wore secondhand clothes, and worked two jobs.

Her embarrassment grew until she felt physically ill. Had these same people who pretended to be her friends at school been making fun of her all along? Val had realized she was in a different socio-economic class than many of her classmates, but this was the first time the division had been made so blatantly clear. Bo and the rich kids in the county lived in a world in which she didn't belong.

The sound of laughter on the beach brought her back to the present. Nearly ten years had passed, and the hurt of that day still stung. She figured that incident was the reason she'd worked so hard to go to school, so she could get out of Millford Creek and prove to everyone she was more than just fun. She didn't want to be someone a man was ashamed to bring home to meet his family.

But the shame that had burned her cheeks all those years ago returned when she heard Candice's words. She was from a different world than Nathaniel, and she hated the feeling her clothing and lack of sophistication would make her an embarrassment.

She pulled a bottle of water out of the ice and twisted off the lid, her gaze traveling over the group.

Over the years, she had spent so much time wishing she could get out of her house and be an independent woman, meeting friends for parties, dating cute guys. She'd dreamt of leaving home, having her own place and not worrying about hurrying back at night to take care of her brothers and sisters. Now that she was here, she realized this wasn't what she wanted at all. The people were friendly...well, most of them. She'd laughed, enjoyed good food, but all she could think about was what she was missing. She should be on the back porch of Couthy Cottage, talking with Nathaniel, or just sitting and not talking at all.

But even that was an illusion. Nathaniel didn't need her company. She would do well to remember she was his temporary employee and not his friend. She walked back through the darkness to the campfire, discovering Brandt and Candice engaged in a rather sloppy make-out session.

When Brandt noticed Val, he stood, swaying. "I missed yah, Val. Where'd yah go?" His voice was loud and his words slurred.

He didn't even have the decency to look embarrassed. "I need to leave, Brandt."

"Already? Gimme a sec to—"

Nothing on heaven or earth would induce Val onto the back of Brandt's motorcycle to drive up a cliffside road. "I'll find a ride. See ya later."

"I'll call yah."

Candice pulled Brandt back down and wrapped her arms around him.

Val left them to their clumsy kissing. She pulled out her phone, wondering if she dared text Nathaniel this late. He would have to wake the kids to come and

70

get her, but the cottage was too far to walk. What other choice did she have? Seth? She dialed Seth's number as she walked to the parking lot, but he didn't answer. Val sighed as she scrolled down to Nathaniel's number and pressed Send.

He answered on the second ring. "Val?"

"Mr. Cavanaugh, I'm so sorry to wake you. I—"

"Val, are you all right? Did he hurt you?"

The concern in his voice brought tightness to her throat. "No, I'm not hurt. But, I need a ride. I'm in the parking lot at Craigwood Beach."

"I'll be right there."

The call disconnected and Val sat on a large rock to wait. She hadn't taken any pain medication for a few hours and the ache of her injuries had returned. She replayed the phone conversation in her mind and her heart did a slow roll as she thought of Nathaniel's words, his voice, how quickly he had pledged to come to her rescue. *Why in the world am I so breathless?* She examined her feelings and stopped quickly, afraid of what she would find, and afraid of the heartbreak the discovery would cause.

Chapter Five

Nathaniel drove down the dark road as quickly as was safely possible, scanning the side of the lane for the Craigwood sign. His heart had pounded steadily for twenty minutes as he envisioned different scenarios that would have led to Val's phone call. His hands shook as he thought of that punk on the motorcycle taking advantage of her. Images filled his mind, and he had to force them out to concentrate on driving. Once he spotted the turn off, he followed the side road to the parking lot, squinting as he searched for Val.

The beams of the headlights swept over the ground and finally illuminated her sitting on a rock near the edge of the lot.

She waved and started toward him.

Nathaniel braked, threw open the door, and sprang out of the car. He grasped Val by the shoulders. "What happened? What did he do to you?" He stepped to the side and tilted his head to get a better look at her face in the light. She looked unharmed, only tired, and cold.

"Nobody hurt me." She squinted and lifted her hand, blinking against the bright lights. "He's drunk. I didn't want to let him drive me home."

The flood of relief that swept over Nathaniel nearly choked him. He released his tensed muscles and wanted nothing more than to pull her into his arms.

Instead, he led her to the passenger side of the car.

He opened the door, reached inside for the blanket she'd gotten after her accident, and wrapped it around her shoulders, and then settled her into the car. Once he'd closed her door, he sagged against it. *Thank goodness, she's okay.* He climbed behind the wheel and turned the car around, heading back to the cottage.

"Mr. Cavanaugh, I am so sorry for dragging you out of bed in the middle of the night. And Finn and Ruby, too." She motioned toward the back seat where his children slept. "I didn't know what else to do…"

"Don't be sorry, Val." He glanced toward where she sat, wrapped in the blanket. Her hair was a mess. "I'd take a midnight drive over another late-night visit from the Highway Patrol any day."

Val formed her mouth into an 'o' and lowered her eyes.

When they arrived at the cottage, Nathaniel lifted Ruby carefully out of her seat. *It's amazing what children can sleep through.*

Val carried Finn

They held the screen door for one another to keep it from banging and tiptoed up the stairs, using hand gestures to communicate as they tucked the kids back in their beds.

Val closed Ruby's door behind her and grinned. "Mission accomplished. Nice work, partner," she whispered.

Even in the shadows her dimples showed. Nathaniel smiled back. He saw the hour was well past midnight, and he was not tired in the least. "I could use some hot chocolate, could you?"

Val nodded. "I'll make it. Let me change first."

"You obviously have no idea how good my hot

chocolate is, or you wouldn't offer."

Her grin grew. "Meet you on the porch then?"

Ten minutes later, Nathaniel carried two cups of thick hot chocolate through the screen door.

Val had changed into pajama pants and a sweatshirt. The blanket was spread across her lap. "Thanks." She took the mug he offered.

The outfit was the most clothing he'd seen her wear at one time. He slid back into the Adirondack chair and watched her, both relieved to have her safe and anxious to see her pleased expression when she tasted the drink. A burst of contentment filled him every time he made her happy, and the confidence in his ability to do something right for a change grew. He realized no matter how hard he'd tried, where Clara was concerned, he'd failed at everything he'd attempted for so long that he'd stopped making any effort.

Val blew across the top of her hot chocolate and took a sip. "Mmmm…"

Nathaniel nodded. "I told you it was good."

"Not just good. Liquid-heaven-in-a-mug good. What's in it?"

"Secret recipe." He wasn't disappointed. It only took the simplest of things to bring utter joy to Val's face and he found the sensation of watching her immensely satisfying.

"And you don't share your secret recipe?"

He shook his head. "I'm taking it to the grave." The crashing of waves soothed him and let him relax as he enjoyed the warm drink. His eyes drifted shut.

"Mr. Cavanaugh?"

With a start, he opened his eyes. "I really think you should call me Nathaniel." He was starting to get drowsy.

"Sir, that would be completely inappropriate, not when I'm working for you."

"That's true, but sometimes you don't seem like an employee."

Val raised her eyes and their gazes met. "I don't act very professional, do I?"

"That's not what I meant. Sometimes, you seem more like a friend." Nathaniel could tell that his guard was down. Why did talking to someone at night free people of their inhibitions? He needed to be careful not to say anything he'd regret.

Val picked at her nails. "I need to thank you again for coming to get me. It's the second time you've rescued me. I'm not doing very well in the whole 'being an independent woman' department, am I?"

"That's what friends do." He closed his eyes and let his head fall back against the chair. Moments later, he sleepily registered Val had moved the blanket to cover him and took the empty mug from his hand, but he was too tired to do more than mutter, "Thanks."

"Good night, Nathaniel."

****

The next morning, Nathaniel walked into the kitchen, massaging his neck as he leaned his head from side to side. He loved the porch chairs, but spending the night in one definitely did his back no favors.

Ruby sat at the table, coloring.

Val stirred something on the stove and held Finn on her hip.

Nathaniel looked over her shoulder before he took his son. "Smells wonderful."

"Daddy sleeping outside," Finn said.

"Y'all sit on down, and breakfast will be ready in a few," Val said.

Nathaniel placed Finn in his booster chair and sat next to Ruby. He leaned his elbows on the table, pushing his fingers through his hair.

"Good morning, Daddy." Ruby looked up from her coloring. "We're having a 'real suthin breakfast'."

"And what is a 'real southern breakfast'?" He smiled a little at his daughter's imitation of Val's accent.

Ruby shrugged.

"Biscuits, gravy, eggs, sausage, bacon, grits." Val set a basket of warm biscuits on the table. "And I cut up some fruit, just in case y'all feel like being healthy." She fixed the children's plates, pouring gravy over their biscuits and cutting up sausage. She lifted a bowl and offered it to him. "Grits, Mr. Cavanaugh?"

"Thank you."

"Do y'all eat a 'real suthin breakfast' every Sunday, Val?" Ruby asked.

Nathaniel cringed a little. He hoped this was just a phase and not a permanent change to Ruby's speech pattern.

"My momma used to make a big breakfast on Sunday. But after she died and my daddy lost his job, we…didn't." She reached to pick up a piece of sausage that had fallen from Finn's plate.

Nathaniel wondered just how hard things had gotten when Val's father was out of work. He watched her pouring juice for the kids and thought about how much of a role she must have played in raising her brothers and sisters. Hadn't she said she had a large family? Why had he never asked her about them before?

"What are we doing today, Daddy?" Ruby asked.

He pulled his thoughts from his nanny and focused on his daughter. "I'm leaving for Boston tomorrow morning, so you and Finn should choose our activities for today."

"I want to see the lighthouse."

"Finn, too." He raised his arms up in the air.

Val lifted Finn out of his booster seat and took him to the sink to wash his hands and face.

"Can Val come with us?" Ruby tugged on his sleeve.

"Certainly, if she wants." He lifted his gaze to meet Val's.

Her brows furrowed and rose the slightest bit.

Nathaniel nodded, smiling to indicate she was welcome to join them. He loved sharing a silent communication with someone. Her smile set off that surge of contentment inside him again.

Val set Finn down and started stacking plates to clear off the table. "I wouldn't miss it, Miss Ruby."

After Nathaniel showered, he drove the four of them out to the point.

A silver-haired man in a flannel shirt met them outside the museum. He introduced himself as K.S. Bennson, the lighthouse keeper, and led them up the winding staircase to the observation deck.

"Look!" Val pointed out at the water.

Nathaniel squinted into the distance and saw a spray of water and the dark shape of a whale as it breeched and re-submerged. A swell grew in his chest. Though he'd seen similar displays often enough, he never failed to marvel at the sight.

"Did you see it?" Val's voice carried a note of delight.

He turned to reply, but saw she was speaking to Ruby. He felt a twinge of disappointment, but pushed it away. He was being ridiculous to assume he was the first person Val would turn to in her excitement. He lifted Finn and stepped closer to watch for the whale again.

K.S. leaned his arms on the rail next to Val. "Nevah get tired of that sight myself."

"I don't imagine ya would." Val smiled.

The lighthouse keeper returned her smile and glanced at the others. "Would yah like a picture of your family?"

Val opened her mouth to reply.

Nathaniel handed K.S. his phone before she could explain their actual relationship. "Thank you." The man didn't need to know every detail about them. He lifted Finn and moved back to stand next to Val."

"Yah better move closer together." He looked at the phone screen and motioned with his hand.

Val caught Nathaniel's gaze and shrugged. Pink spread over her cheeks, but she grinned.

Nathaniel smiled and waggled his brows, causing her to laugh. Joking around with Val felt good. Just as he told her the day before, she seemed more like a friend than an employee. He stood next to her and smiled for the camera, then thanked K.S., and retrieved his phone.

Finn leaned from Nathaniel's arms toward Val. "Go back downstairs now."

She took him from Nathaniel. "I'll take Finn down if y'all want to stay up here a little longer."

"I'm hungry." Ruby pulled on Nathaniel's shirt, her lips turned down at the corners.

He breathed out a sigh and caught Val's gaze again to share a look of pretend frustration at the children's interference. They trooped out to the car. He drove back to the main part of the town. They wandered through the local shops and stopped at Ned's Lobster Shack, sitting at picnic tables while they ate lobster rolls and watched the fishing boats in the harbor.

Nathaniel was fascinated by the way Val interacted with the kids. She never seemed irritated when they wanted her attention. She'd stop what she was doing and listen to any observation, answer any question, no matter how many times they'd asked the same thing before. She seemed to have an endless supply of patience.

Later, the four of them licked ice cream cones as they walked around the Memorial statue of the Lost Fisherman.

He studied the names of the watermen lost at sea engraved at its base while the children played at the park.

Val sat on a bench, watching Finn, and stood a time or two.

Nathaniel figured she was ready to run after him when he chased seagulls. He grinned when he realized he hadn't thought of the caseload once. He'd actually enjoyed an entire day with his family and the stress that typically started his head pounding in the early afternoon was surprisingly missing. He surveyed the park with his hands in his pockets and inhaled a deep breath. *This* is what he'd hoped for when he brought his kids to Maine.

As the afternoon grew later, they strolled out toward the pier where the scales of today's catch glistened in ice chests. The children studied the fish and squealed as the lobsters opened and closed their claws. After an entire day of playing tourist, they all returned to the cottage, exhausted. Val had diligently applied sunscreen to the children, but Nathaniel could feel his arms and neck were sunburned.

Once she'd bathed the kids and tucked them into bed, Val joined Nathaniel on the porch. The sun was nearly gone, and the sky was bathed in a soft glow.

"I have no idea how you do that all day. I am completely exhausted." He stretched out his legs in front of him and rested his head back against the chair.

Val smiled and leaned back against the railing. "You're a fun daddy. Finn and Ruby are lucky to have you."

Her words took him by surprise. He didn't consider himself fun at all, and he was unused to being complimented for his parenting skills. His wife had regularly done the opposite. "I wish I could be with them more. The firm takes up so much of my time."

Val moved to sit in the chair next to him. "They know you love them. And when they're older, they'll realize the reason you work so hard is for them."

"It's not the entire reason." Nathaniel rubbed his palm over his chin. "Some of my professional goals have nothing to do with making myself a better father. And I have days when I've given all I have to my job, and I can't find any more to give when I get home. A lot of guilt comes with juggling a career and family."

"A man who's fulfilled in his work will be happier, and that translates into his relationships with his family.

That's my opinion, anyway. You shouldn't feel guilty or selfish for doing things for yourself." She shrugged. "I guess it's just a matter of balance."

Nathaniel pondered her words. She'd used the term *balance* twice now. Wise advice from someone who had seemingly very little world experience.

Val tipped her head. "From what I've seen, you do it better than most."

"Thank you." He was glad she didn't know the truth. In Boston, he rarely saw his children. A few hours on the weekends were all. He left for the office early and arrived home long after they were in bed. Advancing in his competitive career meant some things had to be sacrificed. He wished he could push away the tight lump of guilt that burned in his chest when he thought of what he was sacrificing.

"Do you like your lawyering job?" Val twisted to face him.

Nathaniel laid his ankle on his other knee. "I forgot, you don't trust lawyers."

"That was last week," Val said. "Now I trust one."

He smiled. Her declaration was so simple, and yet, he felt as if he'd won a victory. He didn't imagine earning Val's trust to be easy, or that she bestowed it often. "You never told me why you don't trust lawyers."

Val looked at him for a moment. "My momma died in a factory accident. Witnesses called it negligence by the company, but in the end, my daddy couldn't afford a lawyer as good as the company's, and the jury determined the accident was her fault."

Nathaniel felt a niggle of conscience. He knew companies hired big-shot lawyers to protect themselves from this exact thing. In fact, he was one of them. The idea that money could buy a verdict didn't sit well, but when a company could afford to appeal again and again, they typically won. "How old were you when your mother died?"

"Ten."

"And you raised your brothers and sisters?"

Val nodded and rubbed her arm.

"Where was your father?"

She looked at him quickly.

But she must have seen his question was asked out of concern instead of accusation, and the defensiveness left her expression.

"After we lost Momma, we watched Daddy change." She pulled her legs up to her chest as she talked, wrapping her arms around her knees. "He stopped smiling and singing. He'd leave for work in the morning, and then come home and go straight to bed. He got so skinny. After a few months, he stopped going to work at all and lost his job. Then, he just shut down. He stopped taking care of us, stopped buying food, and didn't respond when we talked to him. Now, I realize he most likely suffered from depression, but a ten-year-old kid doesn't understand something like that."

She looked toward him again, and then turned her gaze toward the sea in the darkness, letting out a heavy breath. "Not seeing any fireflies here is strange, don't you think? I miss fireflies."

Nathaniel had learned the best way to keep someone talking was not to ask questions, but to wait and allow them to open up at their own pace.

After a few minutes, Val twisted around, leaning her shoulder against the back of the chair. "Since I was the oldest, I cared for the babies. I took money from my daddy's wallet to buy diapers and milk. We ate day-old bread that was thrown away behind the bakery. Every day, I would beg my daddy to eat. When my brothers were old enough to start hunting, they'd bring home whatever they'd killed." She ducked her head. "Sometimes, we sneaked vegetables out of people's gardens."

Val's gaze moved to his and looked away quickly. Her cheeks were flushed. "We were so hungry."

Her whisper was barely loud enough to hear over the waves. He hoped his expression didn't betray his true feelings. His chest heated and his throat was tight. He was angry and completely appalled no one had helped them. "What about your neighbors? Or relatives? Didn't Social Services..." How could a ten-year-old child possibly raise a family and care for a mentally ill father? How had this family been overlooked by the system?

"We have no relatives, and we knew if anyone found out, they'd take us away and give us all to different families."

He couldn't argue with that. "But you wouldn't have been hungry. Everybody would have been taken care of..."

She shifted, lowering her feet to the ground. "Could you imagine Ruby and Finn growing up in different homes? Do you have brothers and sisters?"

"A sister. Rachel."

"What if you were taken away and never saw Rachel again? I was more afraid of losing my family than of starving." She tugged on the hem of her sweatshirt. "I worked at whatever jobs I could find and in time, things got better."

Val somehow managed to sound both vulnerable and strong. "And your father, he's…?"

"In high school, I was in a psychology class. I realized my daddy needed professional help, and I took another job so we could get him seeing a therapist. He's good now." She shook her head. "Not how he used to be, but he works and eats, and sometimes even smiles."

Nausea rolled in his stomach. The expression on her face had been filled with such shame, as if she was worried he'd look down on her for things out of her control. "Val, the fact that you survived, completed school, sacrificed your childhood for your family and saved your dad makes you the strongest person I've ever met."

She lifted her gaze. "I'm not any stronger than anyone else. You never know what you can do until you have to do it. Look at you." She held out her hand toward him. "A young father who lost his wife. You've been through difficult times, too, Nathaniel, and you're working every bit as hard for your family as I worked for mine."

He swallowed hard. If she only knew…he was the last person she should compare herself to, especially regarding the preservation of his family.

For several minutes, they watched in silence as the last flickers of sunlight played off the waves.

From the corner of his eye, he studied Val. "You okay?"

"I've never told that story to anyone before." Val's voice was soft.

"It must be the porch. I've said things out here that I hadn't meant to, as well."

"Next time, it's your turn."

She sounded as if she were trying to make her voice light, but didn't completely succeed. "Thanks for trusting me, Val."

"Thanks for listening."

****

Val was thrilled Nathaniel returned from Boston for the Fourth of July. She and the children had gotten excited for the celebration after they'd gone into town for story time and seen the holiday preparations. Flags and other patriotic decorations hung from balconies and adorned store windows. Booths and carnival rides were being set up in the park by Grant's Lake. Flyers advertising the fireworks show were taped to bulletin boards and the doors of the grocery store.

She prepared a picnic and when Finn woke from his nap, they loaded into the car, and Nathaniel drove them into town. Val had never seen such a large crowd in Lobster Cove. They found a parking place near the movie theater and walked through the vendors, games, and carnival rides.

Val and Nathaniel leaned against the metal rails of the temporary fence surrounding the carousel and waved at the children each time Ruby and Finn came into view.

When she heard someone call their names, Val turned to see Seth striding toward them. A woman walked next to him. Val wondered if she was the only one to notice Nathaniel's brow inched upward when he saw Seth wasn't alone.

"Val, Nathaniel. I'd like you to meet Melanie Owen." Seth grinned.

Nathaniel shook her hand. "Nice to meet you."

"Hi, Melanie." Val smiled and offered her hand. Melanie was small and slender, with light brown hair and hazel eyes. Her greeting was pleasant enough, but Val sensed beneath her friendly exterior, the woman was nervous. Her gaze moved over the crowd and her manners seemed uneasy. She tilted her head as if she was subconsciously hiding her face behind her hair. Val had seen women who'd been mistreated act similarly and wondered about Melanie's history. Was she afraid of something? Or just extremely shy?

"Been here long?" Seth angled his body to include Melanie in their circle.

"Just arrived." Nathaniel lifted a hand to wave at Ruby and Finn as they passed on the carousel.

The other adults followed suit.

"Melanie and I were on our way to set out blankets by the lake. Want us to save you a place for the fireworks?"

"We have a blanket in the car." Nathaniel lifted his chin toward the movie theater. "I'll grab it and help you save some spots." He turned to Val and raised his brows. "If Val doesn't mind me leaving her with the kids on her day off."

"Course not. Go ahead, and we'll catch up when y'all get back."

Seth touched Melanie's arm gently. "Will you be okay here with Val and the kids for a minute or two?"

Melanie nodded. "Sure." She spoke in a voice that was little more than a whisper.

They all lifted their hands when Ruby and Finn passed again, and the men left.

"How'd ya meet Seth?" Val asked, hoping to break through Melanie's shy exterior.

"I work at Sang Freud Coffee House—right next to his clinic."

"You a server?"

Melanie nodded.

"I've put in my share of time waiting tables." Val wrinkled her nose. "Not always the most glamorous job, right?"

Melanie responded with a small smile.

Val wondered what was needed to get this woman to break out of her shell.

When the carousel ride ended, Val and Melanie retrieved Ruby and Finn. They bought the children cotton candy and strolled through the game section of the carnival, watching people competing at the various booths.

Val smiled as she realized how similar the Fourth of July celebration was here on the New England coast to those in the rural Appalachians. She was pulled out of her musings when Ruby squealed, pointing toward a stuffed elephant that hung from one of the carnival booths. "Val, will you get me that elephant, please?"

She looked at Ruby and then raised her gaze to the sign above the game. Shooting gallery. A thrill went through her, and she grinned. "Course I will, Miss Ruby."

The teenage boy running the booth explained how the game worked. Painted targets moved on mechanical tracks. "For each rubber duckie, you get five points, balloons are worth ten. If you hit one of the small targets, your points double." He lifted his hat, shook his longish hair off his forehead, and then crammed the hat back down.

"How many points for that elephant?" Val asked,

pointing toward the pink stuffed animal.

"Two hundred. Good luck."

Val paid a few dollars and took a pellet gun from the boy, hefting it.

He stepped out of the way and put his hand on the start button. "You ready?"

Val lifted the rifle, widening her stance and pulling it against her shoulder as she sighted down the barrel. "Go ahead."

The targets started to move, and Val pulled the trigger. The ping of the pellets striking metal sounded as she hit with each shot, easily passing the two hundred points by the time the music stopped.

"Whoa, you in the army or something?" Wide-eyed, the teen used a long pole with a hook to retrieve the elephant.

"This is how we get supper where I'm from." Val winked, unable to hold back a wide grin. Who knew her skill would ever come in handy for something that didn't involve putting supper on the table?

Melanie laughed quietly, but shook her head when Val offered her the rifle.

"You aiming to try that again, miss?" said a man behind her.

When Val turned, she realized a small crowd had gathered. She noticed Seth and Nathaniel were part of the group, and wondered if Nathaniel had seen her shoot. Did seeing his nanny ace the shooting gallery make him feel impressed or embarrassed?

"Looks like your nanny's attracting some attention." Seth motioned to the people around them.

Val glanced to Nathaniel and smiled. "Anyone else want an elephant?"

"Finn wants a doggy." The boy tugged on her hand.

With a nod, Val reached back into her purse.

Nathaniel pulled out his wallet before she got a chance and handed some bills to the teenager in the hat. He smiled at Val and placed a hand on his hip. "Let's see what you've got, Annie Oakley."

She tossed her ponytail over her shoulder and lifted the rifle. Her heart fluttered slightly, obviously a result of being the center of attention, but she focused on the targets. When the game started, she tuned out the noise of the people around her, and tried to ignore Nathaniel's gaze she could feel without even looking. She squinted down the barrel and pulled the trigger. One by one, the pellets knocked over the moving targets.

When the music finished, the crowd cheered, and the kid handed Finn a stuffed dog.

Nathaniel stepped next to her and bumped her shoulder with his. "Maybe I should have hired you as my bodyguard instead of my nanny."

Val grinned as she handed the pellet gun back to the kid in the hat. "If those rubber duckies were squirrels, we'd be eating good tonight."

He grimaced, wrinkling his nose and showing his teeth.

"Squirrel stew?" Seth threw back his head and laughed. "You can't be serious"

"You city boys don't know what y'all're missing." Val wagged her finger at them.

The group walked away from the shooting gallery and continued through the carnival.

Seth stopped in front of a baseball pitch game and put his hands on his hips. "High school was a long time ago, wasn't it, Nathaniel? Too bad that pitching arm of yours has gone all soft from neglect. I wouldn't want you to hurt yourself with a little friendly competition."

Nathaniel stopped mid-stride and spun, marching toward the booth. "You just talking big, or do you really want me to humiliate you?"

Seth handed a few bills to the man in the booth, and then placed three baseballs on the counter in front of Nathaniel.

Nathaniel tossed a ball in the air and caught it. He turned to Val and Melanie. "Ladies, you might want to cover the children's eyes. They shouldn't have to see their doctor brought to tears." He threw the baseball toward the cutout square next to the picture of a cartoon batter but missed. Narrowing his eyes, he threw the other two and landed one of his three pitches through the hole.

"Looks like the ultimate Red Sox fan suffers from the same problems as his team." Seth laughed at his joke and took a turn, throwing two balls through the strike zone.

Nathaniel slapped a few more bills on the wooden counter and picked up three more balls.

"I think they'll be a while, don't you?" Val said to Melanie. "Let's take the kids somewhere in the shade." She told the men they were leaving, unsure if they even heard, so intent were they upon their competition.

Val bought popsicles for Ruby and Finn, and then led them to a table in the shaded picnic area. "Melanie, I never asked where y'all are from?"

Melanie sat on the bench facing them. "Here and there." She turned her gaze downward. "I lived in Virginia for a little while."

Val thought her answer was strange, but didn't press the issue. If Melanie wasn't comfortable talking about herself, that was her business.

"Back at the shooting booth, Seth said you're Nathaniel's nanny?" Melanie looked up at Val through her lashes.

"Yep." Val lifted Finn onto her lap and leaned back against the table, propping up her feet on the bench next to Melanie. His popsicle dripped down his arm and onto her legs. "I love it. It's the best job I've ever had, and I've worked a lot of jobs."

"Oh, I didn't know. The way you two act together, I thought…" A flush bloomed on Melanie's cheeks.

Val blinked. She opened her mouth and closed it, too surprised to find words.

"I'm sorry." Melanie's flush deepened. "I didn't mean to imply anything."

"No, of course not. I…I mean, I can't believe you thought Mr. Cavanaugh and I…"

"I guess you just get along well." Melanie smiled shyly.

Val took a napkin from the dispenser on the table and wiped at the sticky red streaks on her leg. She wondered if her cheeks were as flushed as Melanie's. "Mr. Cavanaugh's just a really nice person. And I love his kids."

Melanie gazed at Finn and then to Ruby who sat on the other side of Val, swinging her feet and sucking on her popsicle. "I started coaching a kids softball team a few weeks ago," Melanie said in a quiet voice. "I'd never spent much time around children, and had no idea how much I'd love it."

"Yeah, kids can be great, especially these two."

Val ruffled Finn's hair.

"I'd never given much thought to having kids of my own, but now…" Melanie shrugged and smiled. "It doesn't sound so bad."

Melanie's words made Val wonder. Would *she* ever have children? She'd started to think of Ruby and Finn as her own, which she knew was silly. She'd always hoped to be a mother, but the idea of leaving these children in two months was a dreaded thought she wouldn't allow herself to fully form. She was grateful for the arrival of Nathaniel and Seth that pushed away the contemplations before her heart began to ache.

"Daddy, can we have our picnic now?" Ruby asked.

"Sure, we can. Seth found a good spot out by the lake." Nathaniel took Finn and glanced at Val's popsicle-stained legs. His gaze met hers and he smiled.

Bending down her head to cover her blush, Val stood. *Why does his crooked smile have that effect on me?* She took Ruby's hand as they walked toward the picnic blankets.

Something furry brushed against her arm. She looked down, and then took the small stuffed squirrel Nathaniel held toward her. "What's this?"

"I thought you deserved a trophy for your shooting." He met her gaze and quirked his lips in a smile. "As long as you don't try to cook it up."

She would never stop being surprised by the deep blue of his eyes. "I love it." Val ran her finger over the fluffy tail. She was taken aback by the thoughtfulness of the small gift. He'd probably thought of the squirrel as nothing, but she was touched. She couldn't remember anyone doing something so considerate, and for no reason at all.

He bent his arm to the side awkwardly, stretching it as he carried Finn. "I'm glad you like it. That little guy cost me my pride, and I'll be feeling it in my shoulder for a long time."

I wonder how many pitches it took him to win this little squirrel. "As long as you beat Seth, that's what counts, right?"

Nathaniel grimaced. "That's the story I'm sticking to. Don't let him tell you otherwise."

The fireworks display over the Grant's Lake was the most impressive show Val had ever seen, and southerners know a thing or two about explosives. She rested her hands back on the quilt, tilting up her head, and glanced to the side to see Nathaniel watching her. Val smiled, mouthing "what?" as she lifted her shoulders. She was grateful for the darkness that covered the color on her cheeks.

Nathaniel turned his face back toward the glowing sky, but leaned toward her. "Thanks for today."

Even though his arm hadn't touched hers, his nearness warmed the entire side of her body. Val's chest felt like a helium balloon was growing inside. She wished she could think of a way to capture the moment and keep it forever.

Chapter Six

Out of the six weeks Val had been a nanny in Maine, she'd been on her own for almost three of them. Nathaniel had to travel back and forth to Boston more often than he'd planned.

While he was gone, Val and the children played in the park and on the beach. They went to story time at the Cliffside Bookstore and Shuckers Booktique, and a few times rented a movie.

When the weather was bad, they'd explored the attic, finding a hidden panel in the wall and pretending they'd located the entrance to Narnia. They had picnics, ate ice cream, read books, and played, and Val loved every minute of the days. Until the children went to sleep. Then she sat on the porch alone, noticing the absence of fireflies and wishing she had Nathaniel to talk to.

Sometimes, he called to check on the children. She kept him on the phone too long, telling him about their day, asking about his. She knew the lengthy conversations must frustrate him. He was a busy attorney after all, but she looked forward to his phone calls more than anything else.

Brandt and Seth had both contacted her nearly every day. She had no hard feelings toward Brandt, but she told him she didn't have the time to see him with her boss gone. Seth usually called in the evening to make sure everyone was all right. A few times he'd even stopped by with Daisy. Val suspected Nathaniel might have asked him to check on them.

She'd called home a few times a week, but the calls had become shorter as her sisters were both busy with whatever takes up teenage girls' time, and her daddy was never one for long conversations. The realization they had all gone on with their lives and didn't seem to miss her as much as she missed them stung a little.

One warm afternoon, Val, Ruby, and Finn sat outside on a picnic blanket in the shade. Ruby read aloud while Finn slept curled up in Val's lap. Nathaniel had told her the day before if sentencing finished early, he might return before supper. She hadn't wanted to get up the children's hopes. But they baked cookies, and Val wore a new outfit: a t-shirt and knee-length skirt. She didn't want to give any credence to what Clam-Bake Candice had said, but her words had made Val think. After that night, she paid attention to what other women wore around town. She didn't think Nathaniel would notice—or care that she wore something new, but a little part of her hoped.

Ruby finished her book and dug through the basket, choosing a coloring book.

Val shifted Finn off her legs, settling him next to her, and lay down on her stomach, picking up the book she'd borrowed from the Captain's Library. The singing of birds in the forest, the waves crashing, and the cool breeze tempted her to fall asleep, but the purr of an engine caught her attention.

The visitor might be Seth stopping by to check on them, or perhaps Mrs. Spencer. But Val's heartbeat picked up just the same.

Nathaniel's silver car emerged from the forest and pulled into the small garage next to the cottage.

The sight of him walking toward the front porch carrying his suitcase made Val's pulse speed up She was being ridiculous. Was she so desperate for adult company?

Ruby shouted, "Daddy!" and ran to him.

Nathaniel stopped, shading his eyes, and waved when he saw them. Smiling, he swept Ruby into an embrace and carried her toward the blanket.

Val stood to meet him. For an instant, she imagined running into his arms as Ruby had. But shook away the silly thought. "How was your trip?"

Nathaniel glanced at Finn, sleeping on the blanket, and a tired smile tugged at his mouth. He loosened his tie and took off his suit coat. "Good. But I'm glad to be back." He sat next to Val, stretching out his legs and crossing his ankles.

"And you finished gathering your depositions? Or are you still having trouble locating the last witness?"

"I need to be careful what I say. You pay closer attention than I thought." He raised his brows. "Depositions are done, we'll just hope they're enough to keep us out of a trial."

Ruby showed him the books she'd been reading, piling them into his lap.

"And what's this one?" Nathaniel picked up Val's library book, turning it to see the cover. "A biography of Andy Warhol?"

Val reached to take the book. "I saw online the Museum of Fine Art's having a special exhibit of Warhol this fall, and I thought I should brush up on my pop art."

He nodded and met her gaze briefly. "Smart."

Val wished she could read his expression. Her stomach sank at the reminder their situation was temporary. She wondered how Nathaniel felt. Did he feel a twinge of sorrow, too? Or was it 'business as usual, time to hire a new nanny'? The thought of another person moving into her place, living the life she'd started to love, hit her with such force that she gasped.

Nathaniel's gaze snapped to hers. "You okay?"

She nodded, shifting her position. "Must be a stick under the blanket that poked me," she muttered.

"We made cookies, Daddy." Ruby patted his arm.

"Wait here, I'll go get them." Val was on her feet and hurrying to the house before anyone else had a chance to respond. She needed to get a grip on herself. This wasn't her family. Nathaniel wasn't her friend, he was her employer. Ruby and Finn weren't her children. They were her charges.

She blinked away the tears that, despite her chastisement, filled her eyes. *Come on, Val. Focus on your task.* Loading cookies on a plate, grabbing a jug of milk, paper cups and napkins, enjoying the time she had with the Cavanaughs. Worrying about things she couldn't change wouldn't help anything.

That evening, Val put one of Mrs. Spencer's lasagnas in the oven and set out ingredients for a tossed salad. Her phone rang. "Hi, Seth." Val could feel Nathaniel's gaze on her as she listened to his friend.

"Hey, just wanted ya to know a big storm is forecast for tonight. I'm running by in a little while to help fasten the shutters."

"Thank you, but Mr. Cavanaugh's home now.

He'll help me."

"Make sure you have flashlights and batteries."

"Will do, Thanks." She put down the phone and turned to find Nathaniel still watching her. "Seth says a storm's coming tonight. We need to fasten the shutters? I thought those were just for decoration."

He nodded, and they both looked through the window over the sink. The wind had gotten stronger. Trees bent and branches cartwheeled across the ground.

"I'll take care of the shutters." Nathaniel walked in the direction of his bedroom. "Keep the kids inside." He returned a moment later wearing a rain jacket.

"Want some help?" Val asked.

"I don't want you out there either." He opened the back door, letting in a rush of air, and had to use both hands to pull it closed behind him.

He surely hadn't meant anything by his statement, but his words settled around Val like a warm blanket.

****

A loud crash jolted Val out of her sleep. A moment passed before she realized the noise was thunder and louder than any storm she'd heard before. She lay still while her heart pounded. Even with the shutters closed, a flash of lightning set the room aglow, followed by another crash that was, if possible, louder than the first.

The house shook and groaned. The wind sounded like a shriek.

Val wasn't one to be afraid during a thunderstorm, but she'd never experienced anything like this. How were the kids still sleeping?

As if in answer to her question, she tensed at the sound of Ruby's terrified scream.

Val bolted from her room and crossed the hall.

"Ruby, I'm here." She ran her hand up the wall next to the door, locating the light switch, but when she toggled it, nothing happened. With hands outstretched, she hurried to the bed.

Ruby clung tight. "Val, I'm scared."

"I won't leave you. Come on, let's check on Finn." She carried Ruby into the dark hall, and they both cringed when another crash shook the house.

"Daddy?" Finn cried out.

"Val?" Nathaniel's voice sounded from the stairs. The beam of a flashlight lit up the hallway

"I'm here. I have Ruby."

He moved past her into Finn's room, and returned carrying the boy.

Both children continued to cry, and the wind howled. Something crashed against the house.

"Let's take them downstairs." Nathaniel found Val's hand.

She shifted Ruby onto her hip.

Nathaniel's hand was strong and warm and she hadn't realized how nervous the storm had made her until she felt his unspoken comfort. They made their way down the stairs to the living room. He released her hand as he settled the three of them on the couch.

Val immediately felt the loss of his warm touch.

Nathaniel left for a moment and returned with a quilt, covering the four of them.

Finn still cried, and Val snuggled him in her lap.

Ruby climbed into Nathaniel's. "Daddy, I'm scared."

"Don't worry. Go back to sleep now. Val and I won't leave you." Another crash shook the house, and Nathaniel startled.

"Don't you go getting scared on me, too. You're the only thing keeping me from hiding under my bed." Val heard her own whispered voice trembling.

Again, Nathaniel found her hand, and warmth flowed up her arm.

She leaned her head against his shoulder. Cocooned in the warmth of the blanket while the elements raged outside, Val had never felt so safe. She tried to enjoy the sensation, but she felt her stomach sinking. What was she doing? Did she really think he considered her part of his family?

The memory of Bo Callaway's words in the high school hallway floated into her mind, and her insides twisted into a tight ball. Was she really letting herself again develop feelings for a person who was so out of her reach? Hadn't she learned her lesson the first time? She was setting herself up for heartache and needed to figure out how to put distance between herself and the Cavanaughs, especially Nathaniel. Either that or have her heart broken when she left in six weeks. Maybe she'd call Brandt tomorrow and see what he and his friends were doing.

Thoughts of spending another day with the group left her feeling unsettled. She should be excited. Brandt and his friends were fun, and she was a young single woman living on her own for the first time in her life. She should want to hang out with other people in her situation.

Val had a harder time directing her thoughts as sleep crept closer. No matter what happened in the future, she had this moment right now. She'd enjoy it while it lasted.

****

For a long time, Nathaniel didn't fall asleep, and he couldn't blame his wakefulness on the furious storm. Nor could he fault discomfort. He couldn't remember a time when he'd felt quite so content. He was warm and snug, bundled with his children in the dark. Yet, his entire body was alert—hyper-focused on the woman leaning against his shoulder.

The feel of Val moving or squeezing his hand caused every nerve ending to tingle. He listened to her breathing and identified the exact moment when she fell asleep. Knowing she felt protected and comfortable enough to sleep against him during a terrifying storm spread heat through his chest. He hadn't had such intimate physical contact with a woman in years. His wife had been the opposite of warm and tender. He didn't realize how much he craved the feeling.

Probably time to start dating again. But the thought didn't hold any interest. Meeting new people, spending the time to get to know them, hoping they liked his children. The entire process sounded exhausting, when what he really wanted was much simpler. He wanted this. Home, Family. People that cared for him and comforted him. Somehow, Val had become part of it.

He thought of their phone calls and texts over the past weeks. He'd looked forward to the sound of her voice as much as his own children's. Their conversations had run the gamut between playful and serious. She was interested in his work and listened to details of cases she had no doubt found boring. Her questions indicated she listened and put thought into the things he said. He always hung up the phone in high spirits. The interactions had become addicting. He'd forced himself to restrict the number of calls. Val, of course, didn't want to talk to him as often as he'd wanted to talk to her.

When summer ended, he would miss their friendship, probably as much as Ruby and Finn would. His chest tightened at the thought and he pushed it away, focusing on here and now. Thinking about how it felt to have a partner, a friend, someone to hold his hand in the middle of the night and listen to his day. He shifted and Val sighed, nestling against him. *Will my life ever have another moment as perfect as this one?*

****

The next morning, Nathaniel walked around the outside of the house, opening the shutters and surveying the damage. A few shingles had been lost, the deck chairs were piled against one railing, and the yard was littered with sticks and other debris.

While he righted the wooden chairs, he answered a call. A client, Lamar Dunford, would be in town for the day and hoped to meet in Lobster Cove for a business lunch.

When Nathaniel asked Val about switching her day off, she apologized but told him she'd already made plans with friends. He'd been surprised, but her explanation was perfectly reasonable. He hadn't asked with whom, and she hadn't offered the information. The conversation was entirely appropriate for an employee-employer relationship. But he couldn't for the life of him stop wondering who she was meeting, and wishing the question didn't bother him. Better not be the jerk with the motorcycle who was drunk at Craigwood Beach. Did Val still see that guy?

He placed a call to Mrs. Spencer who agreed to

watch Ruby and Finn for a few hours. Nathaniel picked up Lamar Dunford in the center of town to drive out to the Mariner's Fish Fry.

The meeting was productive, and actually rather enjoyable as they hammered out the details of their defense strategy. Lamar was a red-faced, blustering man who gave the impression of being constantly irritated. The first time they met, Nathaniel had been wary. Mr. Dunford was the kind of person juries didn't relate with at all. But as they'd spent time together, Nathaniel had come to see beneath his gruff exterior and realized Lamar was honest and meticulous in his documentation and work. A dream client.

Nathaniel drove Mr. Dunford back into town and insisted he try a blueberry tart from Julie's sweet shop before he returned to Boston. He held open the glass door, glancing at the flyer for the Lobster Cove Trawlers softball team, and waited as a group walked out. Out of the corner of his eye, he saw Mr. Dunford step back to allow a woman to pass by them on the sidewalk.

"Excuse me," she said.

When he heard her voice, Nathaniel released the door and turned quickly. "Val?" He glanced behind her, but she was alone. Had she lied about meeting friends?

Val carried a bag with a rolled-up beach towel and the Andy Warhol book inside. She wore a tank top and shorts, with the strap of a swimsuit evident at her shoulder. She stopped on the sidewalk and met his gaze with brows drawn together.

She looked as if she was unsure whether she should approach him when he had a client. Nathaniel held out a hand. "Val, I'd like you to meet Mr. Dunford."

Val took a step closer and smiled shyly. "How do ya do?"

"This is Valdosta McKinley, my nanny."

Lamar held out his hand. "Your nanny? Where are you from, Miss McKinley? Did I detect a southern drawl?"

"West Virginia. A small town called Millford Creek."

"I have a soft spot for southern belles." He shook Val's hand and placed his other on top of hers, drawing her closer and smiling kindly. "What brings you into town today?"

"I'm a little early to meet some friends, and I thought I'd stop in at the gallery." She indicated the building next to the sweet shop.

"Val's an art historian." Nathaniel hoped Lamar wouldn't ask further about her credentials.

Lamar released Val's hand and looked behind her at the windows of The Venus Gallery. "I never could understand what people see in that modern art. Looks like something a kindergartener painted with his fingers."

Val's eyebrows rose along with her chin. "Maybe y'all just need a little lesson? Come on inside, and I'll show ya around." She glanced at Nathaniel and squinted her eyes. "That is if you're not in a hurry."

"I always have time for a lovely young lady." Lamar stepped past her and opened the gallery door. "After you, Miss."

"Too bad the gallery doesn't typically have much modern art here," Val said when she entered.

Nathaniel followed them through the door. After the noise and bustle of the street outside, the quiet of the space closed around him, and he couldn't help but feel calm.

Two women stood at the register. When the group entered, they turned and looked toward the door.

As he wondered what they would say to Val, Nathaniel's calmness disappeared. Would they be patronizing because of her clothing? His shoulders tightened as one of the women approached.

"Afternoon, Abby," Val said.

"Hi, Val. You've come to admire the Copeland again?"

"Course I did." She smiled and then turned to include the men in the conversation. "Mr. Dunford, Mr. Cavanaugh, this is Abigail Longley, one of the owners of The Venus Gallery."

"Nice to meet you." The tall woman with long strawberry blonde hair smiled, glancing between the men. "Is there something I can help you gentlemen find?"

"I wanted to show them a few of your pieces, if that's all right?" Val tipped her head toward the back of the gallery.

Abby nodded. "Let me know if you have any questions." She walked back toward the register.

Nathaniel's shoulders relaxed. Apparently, Val had been here before. He wondered what the Longley woman meant by the Copeland.

Val led them to a partitioned section of the gallery with brightly colored paintings on each wall. Track lighting focused on each picture. "These pieces were all painted by an artist from Italy, Mariano Pulido. He is known for bright colors and movement in his work."

Nathaniel couldn't help but be impressed. This

didn't sound like the same woman in the ripped skirt that had told him about getting arrested for skinny-dipping in her high school pool. She knew what she was talking about and spoke with confidence.

"See what I mean?" Lamar pointed at a painting. "This doesn't even look like a horse. My grandson could do a better job."

Val took Lamar's arm and turned him to face the picture directly. "If you want a perfect reproduction of a horse, you'd buy a photograph. What's amazing about this painting is you can tell it's a horse, even when the picture doesn't look at all like one. See what I'm saying?"

Eyes wide, Lamar looked at her and then back at the painting.

She traced the shape in the painting with her hand movement. "The artist is showing what horse-ness is. He intends you to *feel* the horse, not just see it. You can hear the wind flowing through the mane, feel the pounding of hooves as it runs, the strain of muscles in its withers…"

He turned back, his head tilted and his nose wrinkled.

Nathaniel's protectiveness returned, and he nearly intervened.

"If you don't feel it, this painting isn't the one for you. Not everyone connects with every piece of art. Let's try another." Val gave a gentle tug on Lamar's arm and led him to the next wall where they stood in front of a mass of colorful swirls and whorls.

"Now, this just plain doesn't look like anything," Lamar said, shaking his head.

"Remember, you need to use all your senses, not

just your eyes. Give it a second." Val spoke in a low voice. "You need to open your mind in order to feel what the artist is trying to show you."

Lamar stared at the picture.

Nathaniel was impressed with what a good sport he was being.

"Maybe it reminds you of an old quilt." Val moved her hand in front of her like she was washing a window. "Or colorful candies, or an oil spot in water. Maybe—"

"Clouds." Lamar interrupted. "It's the sky with wind blowing the clouds in different shapes." His body tilted slightly forward as he stared at the painting. "On my grandfather's farm, lying in the old hammock, I'd watch the clouds…" He spoke in a faraway voice.

The corners of Val's mouth turned down, and her brows rose as she looked at Nathaniel.

He smiled back and lifted his shoulders.

"The corn rustled in the fields, the air sometimes smelled like smoke, Grandmother made lemonade." Lamar gazed at the painting, his mouth slightly open, and suddenly he blinked, pulling back his head. He looked at Val.

"You did it, Mr. Dunford." She patted his arm and smiled.

Nathaniel didn't know how Lamar could possibly continue to stare at the painting when Val's dimples were every bit as enchanting as any piece of art he'd ever seen.

Lamar turned to the plaque next to the painting, reading the name of the piece and a small biography about the artist.

Nathaniel thought Lamar would balk at the price and want to get on their way, but he stayed, content to study the picture.

Val stepped closer to Nathaniel, motioning him away with a tip of her head. "I think we should give him some privacy, don't you?"

Lamar didn't even seem to notice them leave.

Nathaniel watched Val as she studied some of the other works. She'd look at them for a moment, take a step back and allow her gaze to travel over the entire canvas. She never hurried past a painting, or a sculpture, taking the time to appreciate each in turn. He finally broke the silence. "What is the Copeland?"

A slow smile swept across Val's face as she glanced toward the other side of the gallery. "Ryan Copeland's the artist's name. I always save that one for last. It's my favorite." She led him toward the far wall where a large painting hung.

The picture was nearly six feet across and was of a lighthouse on a point above a small village. Wisps of fog covered the scene, and a beam shone from the top of the lighthouse out toward the sea. The waves were choppy. He could just see a ship in the distance, nearly completely hidden in the darkness.

The scene was gloomy and forlorn, and the theme nothing unusual. Nathaniel had seen probably a hundred paintings just like this around town. He wondered what Val saw in this one. Others were surely more beautiful and cheerful. When he looked at her face, he was surprised by her expression. Her gaze moved across the canvas, and her eyes shone with a light he couldn't put into words, but tugged at something deep inside him.

"Not Forgotten" was the title on the plaque next to the piece, and beneath it, a price tag that left no doubt as to why this painting hadn't been taken home by a tourist. Even one with a thick wallet.

Val watched him with her eyes squinted. "What do y'all think?"

His mind scrambled to think of something to say. "It's nice. The lighthouse beam will keep the ship from crashing into the rocks. The sailors are lucky the lighthouse workers keep it running, even in the terrible storm." He felt as though he'd feigned understanding of the piece about as well as he had during his art appreciation classes in school. He'd given a good interpretation, he was certain, although he still couldn't see what Val loved about it.

She looked at him through half-lowered lids for a moment.

He got the impression she could see through his sham of an art critique.

She pointed at the rocky cliff beneath the lighthouse. "Look at the houses. One has a glowing window, as if someone is still awake and waiting. Probably waiting for one of the sailors. Someone is hoping he comes home safely." She looked away.

He had to strain to hear her voice.

"I guess that's why this piece is so special to me. We all hope no matter how far we go, or what we do in life, someone is thinking of us. Might be because I'm so far from home, and I go days without hearing from my family."

"You're not forgotten, Val." He brushed his finger on her arm. "Not by your family, not by anyone who's met you."

She pulled away her arm.

Odd. He wondered if he had said something wrong.

"Maybe not yet."

She spoke so softly that Nathaniel wondered if he'd even heard her correctly.

Val looked at her watch and then toward the door. "I need to get going. Please tell Mr. Dunford I hope he enjoyed the art. I don't want to bother him." She pulled the bag onto her shoulder and waved at Abby as she hurried out the door.

Nathaniel stared at the painting. He looked at the glowing window in the little house. That one smudge of yellow paint pulled at his heart. He thought of all the times he'd come home to his house in Boston, only to find the house dark, the children asleep and Clara out, who knows where. He'd known the feeling of being forgotten.

But then his mind turned to yesterday when he'd returned to the cottage. Val and the children had been delighted to see him. Ruby had run to him. Val had made cookies, and even worn a new outfit. Though he wouldn't delude himself and believe she'd worn it for him. When she saw him, her face had lit up, and the stress of a long week in court had evaporated.

Val would leave on the light while his ship sailed home. He rolled his eyes and pushed away the trite thoughts. He felt ridiculous at getting so wrapped up in a piece of art. He rejoined Lamar who left the gallery an hour later, the proud owner of two new paintings, and a few thousand dollars lighter.

Once he said good bye to his client, he stopped at Julie's Sweet Shop to buy two lobster-shaped sugar cookies for Ruby and Finn and walked back to his car. He pulled onto Maple Avenue, tempted to drive out to the beach to check on Val, but instead, turned the wheel in the other direction and headed for the cottage.

His phone rang. When he saw the name of his mother-in-law—*Was she still his mother-in-law?*—he almost didn't answer. But he knew Marielle would just continue to call, and he might as well get it over with. "Hello, Cavanaugh speaking."

"Nathaniel, how are things going up there? How are my grandchildren?"

"Ruby and Finn are doing well, and we're enjoying ourselves."

"We wondered if the children could spend a few days with us. Lawrence and I can bring them back when we come up to Lobster Cove this weekend."

If Nathaniel hadn't been at a stop sign, he might have swerved off the road. They were coming to Lobster Cove?

"Could you bring them down Wednesday? I'm just dying to spend time with my grandbabies."

The pout in her voice sounded so much like his late wife's that his stomach soured. But he knew Ruby and Finn would love to spend a few days with their grandparents. "I'll bring them Wednesday. You'll be coming back up here on Friday or Saturday?" That would give Ruby and Finn two or three nights. The perfect amount of time. Much more and he thought they'd get homesick.

"Do you have someone to watch them? A nanny you could send?"

He tightened his grip on the steering wheel. No way would he leave Val in the clutches of Marielle Lassiter. Just the thought of how the woman would treat her made Nathaniel want to keep Val as far away from his mother-in-law as possible. His kids were a different story. Their grandmother would treat them well—dote on them—for short spells at a time. She'd want to bring them downstairs to show them off to her bridge club or Lawrence's golf buddies and then send them back to play with the nanny. She would spoil them for a few days, and they'd be on their way. They were her grandchildren, after all, and she should have them visit. The Boston Agency he'd used before will have a competent caregiver.

"I'll find someone."

"Perfect. We'll see you Wednesday."

Chapter Seven

Val was so lonely she thought she'd cry. She'd never in her life spent so much time by herself. Two days ago, Nathaniel had taken Ruby and Finn to Boston. They were due back tomorrow, but the time had crawled by.

She'd been to the beach and a few galleries in Bar Harbor, rented some movies, and read a few books. Mrs. Spencer had come out to clean the house, and Val followed her around like a puppy. The silence in Couthy Cottage was so heavy she thought she could take a bite out of it. She'd definitely been alone too long and decided to stop feeling sorry for herself. She'd do what all southern women did.

Val headed into town, to the grocery mart, in search of comfort food. She perused the aisles, looking for anything that reminded her of home. Finally, she made her purchases, and then returned to the cottage with bags full of groceries to start cooking.

She found a country station on the radio in the kitchen and turned it up, chasing away the silence with the sweet tones of George Strait. She mixed cornbread, mashed potatoes, made coleslaw, boiled macaroni, and while she was waiting for the oil to heat, started breading the steaks. A blop of egg dripped onto her foot.

Val cursed and hopped to the sink, turning on the

faucet with her forearms since her hands were covered in the thick breading mixture, and stuck her foot—flip-flop and all—under the water. She stretched her arm toward the dishtowel, wishing she'd grabbed it before putting her foot in the sink. She glanced up and saw the towel Nathaniel extended toward her.

A smile pulled at one side of his mouth.

Heat flooded Val's face. "Mr. Cavanaugh, you're not supposed to be home until tomorrow." She turned off the water and dried off her foot as gracefully as she could under the circumstances.

"Most of the office took tomorrow off, and I didn't particularly care to spend the day with my...children's grandparents. Sorry if I interrupted." He gestured toward the food preparation. "Are you expecting someone?"

Val returned to the stove, placing the steaks in the hot oil and then washing the floury paste off her fingers. "You shouldn't apologize for coming to your own house. And no. I'm not expecting anyone."

"You have enough food here to feed a small country. Are you telling me you made all of this for yourself?" He lowered his head and moved his gaze from her to the enormous mess in his beautiful kitchen.

"Unless y'all care to join me."

The other side of his mouth lifted. "I'd love to."

"Then go change out of those nice clothes. I should have all this ready in about twenty minutes." Val turned down the music and hurried to put the dirty bowls and dishes into the sink.

Moments later, he returned wearing jeans and a button-down shirt and leaned his shoulder against the doorframe. "Anything I can do to help?"

Val wished he wouldn't watch her with such an intense gaze. She bent over to pull the cornbread out of the oven and felt her skin heat again. *Is his shirt the exact blue of his eyes?* "No. Just sit on down. I'll be right over. *Why didn't I wear my new skirt today?*

Nathaniel carried some of the dishes to the table. "Dinner smells good. What southern delicacy did you make tonight?"

She pulled a bottle of the local Lighthouse Lager he liked so much out of the fridge and used it to point to the dish he was holding. "That there's some possum I scraped off the road."

Nathaniel blanched and looked down at the chicken fried steak.

Val took the plate from him and set it on the table then swatted at his chest. "I'm teasing. I don't think y'all even have possum up here. I got everything at the grocery store, so don't ya worry now."

He twisted his lips in a smile and shook his head. He pulled off the cap of his beer and took a long drink.

Val watched as he ate, nervous when he'd try a new dish and relieved at the look on his face when he told her how much he liked everything. The comfort food did exactly what it was intended to, giving her that feeling of well-being that comes from fried food and good company. "I searched for turnip greens, but the Lobster Cove grocery mart doesn't have the same produce as Winn-Dixie."

"I don't know how you eat like this and stay so small." He leaned back in his chair and finished his drink, then went to the fridge for another.

While Val cleared the plates, he tied a dish towel around his waist like an apron and rolled up his sleeves.

Clean up took only twenty minutes, and they moved out to the porch. Crickets chirped and the waves crashed on the cliffs. The hour was much later than their usual time on the porch, and the night was fully dark.

"How was Boston?" Val asked.

He shrugged and settled back into the chair. "You don't want to hear about hours of meetings, going over briefs and depositions. Boston was all a whole lot of the same."

"I like hearing about your work. And it wasn't the same. You and the kids visited their grandparents this week." She crossed her arms. "Are Ruby and Finn having a good time? I miss them like crazy."

"Yeah, I'm sure Marielle and Lawrence are spoiling them now, but they'll be glad to bring the children home tomorrow."

"I bet seeing their grandkids is good for them. They must miss their daughter terribly."

Nathaniel turned toward her, his face awash in shadow.

She wished she could see his expression. "Is visiting difficult for you? Spending time with them must remind you of your wife."

He let out a breath. "It's difficult, but not for the reasons you're thinking."

"I'm sorry your loss still hurts you so badly."

He walked to the railing, leaning his forearms against it.

Val thought she must have said too much. His wounds over his wife's death ran too deep. Why did she go and make it worse? Her heart ached for the pain he was undoubtedly suffering. The crash of the waves seemed to grow louder as the silence stretched. Val had almost decided the conversation was over when Nathaniel turned to face her. She could only see his silhouette.

He finished his drink and set the bottle on the railing. "Val, a couple weeks ago when we sat out here you told me something you'd never told anyone. I could blame the darkness, or the fact you're a good listener, or the closest thing I've had to a friend in years besides Seth." He raked his hands through his hair. "Or else I'll blame the beer, or maybe you looking at me like I'm some sort of hero, raising my kids alone. I can't take it anymore." He crossed his arms over his chest. "So, here's the truth."

Val sat still. The air was heavy, and she twisted a lock of hair. What was he going to tell her? Every time she heard him speak of his wife, she hated her resentment toward the woman. How could she feel like that about someone who was dead? And a mother besides?

"Val, my marriage wasn't great. It wasn't even good." He cleared his throat. "The relationship was eight years of hell." He let out a ragged breath. "Clara and I met in college and got married too young. I was excited for a family. She was excited to have a fancy wedding. At first, we both wanted the same things. At least I thought we did, but as the years passed, we grew apart. Not just grew apart. We fought all the time. And when we weren't fighting, we avoided each other. We'd go weeks without speaking. My own home became a place I dreaded. If not for Ruby and Finn, I wouldn't have even suggested we try therapy."

"You did your best. Things don't always—"

"I didn't do my best." He spoke in a loud voice,

smacking his hand against the railing and sending the bottle clattering onto the wooden boards. "I wanted out. Clara died the same night I served her with divorce papers. She stormed out of the house without looking back. A few hours later, two highway troopers appeared on my porch. Some hero I am."

Val stood and leaned against the balcony next to him. Her throat ached. "Oh, Nathaniel, I am so sorry."

He turned toward her, his hand on the railing. "Stop saying that. Everyone has said that to me for the past nine months. If they only knew the truth. I don't hurt. I don't feel anything, and that's even worse. I took my kids' mother away from them, and I don't even feel sorry."

"But you can't blame yourself." Val touched her fingers on his arm. It shook. "You must see that. The accident wasn't because of you."

He grabbed onto her hand. "You don't even understand. You're young and innocent, always happy, always helping. You saved your family, you saved Finn. I destroyed mine." He dropped his head. "I'm a monster."

His tight grip was painful. Val reached for his other hand, brushing her fingers down his arm until she clasped it. "If I didn't have this job, I'd be homeless and broke. You gave me a chance to follow my dream." She threaded her fingers through his, hoping he could see the truth in her words. That he could feel how much she meant them. "You're not a monster. You saved *me*."

Nathaniel took a step closer, pulling her toward him. He slid his hand beneath her ear, around the back of her neck and cupped her head, lifting her face until their lips met. His other arm pressed against her back, pushing her against him.

Val threaded her fingers into his hair, and he tilted his head to deepen the kiss. Her knees were weak and her heart pounded. Nathaniel's arms were strong, his lips tender, and she thought she might melt through the boards of the deck. He pulled away but she still felt her pulse in her lips. She opened her eyes slowly, savoring the moment and brushed her thumbs along his scratchy jaw line, sighing and leaning her cheek against his chest.

Nathaniel tensed, his arms dropped, and he stepped from her embrace. "Val, I'm sorry. That was uncalled for. I was caught up in my emotions. I shouldn't have…I'm sorry."

Val's body went rigid and her throat squeezed until she thought she couldn't breathe. Tears stung her eyes, and she was grateful for the darkness. She knew she should say something. She should act as if the kiss had been a mistake and she regretted it, but nothing could be farther from the truth. Nathaniel's kiss had set her blood on fire. In his arms, she'd felt like she belonged, that she'd found her other half, and she'd thought he felt the same.

But she was wrong. Just like she'd been with Bo Callaway. She gripped the railing. She wasn't the kind of girl a man like Nathaniel would be interested in. And the rejection stung every bit as badly as when she was in high school. She didn't trust herself to speak and fought to hold in her sobs as she fled into the house.

****

As they ran the next morning, Nathaniel could feel Seth studying him. His friend could obviously tell

119

something was the matter, but Nathaniel wasn't revealing anything about the night before. He didn't understand his own feelings over what had happened between him and Val.

The softness of her hands, the conviction in her voice when she'd defended and reassured him Clara's death wasn't his fault. She actually believed it. Actually believed in him. Telling her the truth had felt like the exact right thing to do. Kissing Val had felt like coming home. Just the thought of their closeness hours later shot heat through his body. He'd trusted her with the deepest, most secret parts of himself and instead of shying away, Val had responded with understanding and acceptance.

Only when his brain kicked in had he realized what he'd done. What they were doing, and he'd had to stop it. He knew he'd hurt her. The person who'd listened and comforted him. Even in the darkness, he could feel her distress. But what other choice did he have? He couldn't treat Val like a summer fling. She deserved better.

Seth continued to regard him with a questioning expression while they stretched out at the old fence. "You sure nothing's wrong?"

"Everything's fine."

"How's Val?"

Nathaniel shot a dark gaze toward Seth.

Seth nodded. "I thought that was it." He pushed on the fence, leaning forward to stretch out his calves.

"What does that mean?"

"Means I can tell something's going on between you two." Seth traded legs and leaned forward again. "I knew you the whole time you were with Clara, and I never saw you look at her the way you look at Val." He stood on one leg, shaking out the other, and then switched. "Just the way you're acting right now tells me more is there than you want people to think."

Nathaniel leaned back against the rails, crossing his arms. "And what am I supposed to do? She leaves in a few weeks. Not to mention, Val and I are from completely different worlds."

"Last time I checked, you were both from planet Earth."

Nathaniel stayed silent.

"You want my diagnosis?"

"Are you a psychologist now?" Nathaniel furrowed his fingers through his hair.

"You've been beating yourself up about Clara for years now. Not just her death, which was in no way your fault. You feel responsible for the problems in your marriage, and in some weird way you're punishing yourself." Seth walked around the fence to face his friend. "You do deserve to be happy. And if Val makes you happy…"

Nathaniel's jaw tightened. "Then what? I keep her from her dream in Paris? Take her to Boston where she'll feel completely lost?"

Seth opened his mouth to speak.

With a wave, Nathaniel cut him off. "Listen, the kids' grandparents will be here for dinner on Sunday. You want to come?"

"Marielle and Lawrence?" Seth's mouth turned downward. "Should be interesting."

Interesting was an understatement. "Is that a yes?"

"One might wonder whether you are inviting me to ease some of the awkwardness, or if it's my world-famous grilled salmon you're after."

Nathaniel sighed and tipped his head. "It's both"

"You sure do know how to make a guy feel wanted."

The man's ego was unbelievable. Nathaniel rolled his eyes.

"Mind if I bring Melanie?"

The mention of Seth's friend was just a reminder of how caught up Nathaniel had been in his own problems for the last few months. He didn't know anything about this woman his friend was apparently seeing. "You don't think Marielle and Lawrence will scare her away? She seemed pretty shy."

"Nah. And she likes Val." He smirked. "She came right out and admitted it. Imagine that."

Nathaniel muttered something that resembled a farewell and walked up the road to the cottage.

He grabbed a water bottle from the fridge and noticed a spoon in the sink. Val must have had breakfast. She wasn't on the back porch. Maybe in her room? Or she may have gone for a walk. He didn't blame her for avoiding him.

He showered and worked in his office for the majority of the day, thinking of what Seth had said. His thoughts turning more often than they should to Val. Should he check on her? He started up the stairs half a dozen times before talking himself out of it. What would he say? Apologize again for kissing her? Ask if she felt better today after she'd fled in tears?

He couldn't think of anything that wouldn't simply dredge up injured feelings. He'd probably make it worse. Or downplay the moment, which would be more hurtful. In the end, he stayed in his office, straining for sounds coming from the floor above.

Later that afternoon, Nathaniel heard the crunch of gravel beneath tires and hurried outside as his in-laws pulled in front of the house.

Ruby opened her door and ran toward him as soon as the car stopped. "Daddy!" She squeezed her arms around his waist and looked past him to the door. "Where's Val?"

Finn strained against the straps of his car seat and held onto Nathaniel's neck when he was finally freed. "Daddy. We home!" The boy leaned and squirmed, indicating he wanted to be put down. "Val!"

Hearing her name, Nathaniel turned his head and saw Val kneeling on the steps, smiling and nodding as she listened to Ruby jabber away about her trip to her grandparents' house. She wore a short lightweight cotton sundress held up with thin lacy straps.

Finn joined them, and Val pulled him into her lap as she continued to listen to Ruby.

"So that's the famous 'Val' we heard about for the last two days." Lawrence joined Nathaniel and let out a low whistle.

Nathaniel didn't acknowledge the man's reaction with a response. Instead, he opened the car door for Marielle.

His mother-in-law was applying lipstick and turned her head back and forth to study the effect before she closed her mirror and returned it to her purse. Without looking, she reached out a hand for Nathaniel to assist her from the car. She stepped out and allowed her gaze to travel over the scene, taking in the cliffs, the yard, and finally the cottage. "Oh really, Nathaniel. I didn't know you were *camping* out here. Why not take the children to a nice resort?" She took a step toward the house but when her gaze landed on Val, she froze.

Nathaniel actually saw her nostrils flare, and a surge of protectiveness rose inside him. He walked to the steps. "Val, come meet Finn and Ruby's grandparents."

Her gaze met his briefly, but she turned away, lifting Finn and holding onto Ruby's hand as she joined him on the gravel drive.

At the sight of her red puffy eyes, Nathaniel drew in a breath, his stomach sinking. He saw Marielle look Val up and down and fought against the impulse to shield his nanny from her scrutiny. "Val, I'd like you to meet Mr. and Mrs. Lassiter. Marielle and Lawrence, this is Valdosta McKinley."

"Valdosta?" Lawrence's eyebrow rose.

"Pleased to meet you, Mr. and Mrs. Lassiter." Val held out her hand.

"My goodness, have some decency and put on some clothes." Marielle pointed toward the door.

Val blinked. She opened her mouth and took a step back. Red flooded her cheeks as she glanced down at the yellow sun dress.

He hadn't seen it before so Nathaniel was sure she'd chosen the dress especially for the occasion.

"Marielle." Nathaniel stepped between them, taking his mother-in-law's arm. "You haven't seen the view from the porch."

"Is this why you didn't send her down to Boston? That woman is wearing little more than a negligee."

Nathaniel shook, furious that Marielle would insult Val. The look of humiliation on Val's face hurt like a punch in the gut.

"I won't have a woman like her around my grandchildren. Do you want Ruby to think it's okay to dress like a call girl?" She curled her lip and wrinkled her nose.

The edges of Nathaniel's vision turned red. He didn't think he'd ever been so fiercely angry in his life. He wanted to squeeze Marielle's bony elbow until she screamed. Her voice sounding every bit as arrogant as Clara's made it all the worse.

"Marielle—" He was impressed he could make his voice sound as calm as it did. "—Miss McKinley is my employee and my friend. She saved Finn's life at personal risk to her own. She is the kindest, most genuine person I've ever met. I don't care what she chooses to wear because I know she loves my children, and that's what's important."

The screen door closed behind him.

Marielle's eyes narrowed and she darted a look back at the cottage. "What's really going on up here? Nathaniel, what are you doing with that woman?"

"That's enough talk about the nanny." Lawrence flicked his hand.

He finally must have decided to intervene before things got ugly.

Lawrence took his wife's arm. "Nathaniel, why don't you show us your vacation home? And Marielle and I were hoping to take you out to dinner. We heard The Cliffside, next to our hotel, is supposed to be one of the best places in town."

"That will be fine." Nathaniel held up a hand, palm forward. "But let me just be clear. I won't tolerate any ill speaking of Val under my roof. Such behavior is completely unacceptable, and I refuse to allow that sort of talk to reach my children's ears."

Both Lawrence and Marielle stared.

He was sure they'd never heard him put his foot down. He'd certainly never stood up to his wife. Nathaniel was glad he'd not just let the incident slide. Val needed a defender, and he was the only one who could do it. If only he'd found his backbone a few years earlier when Clara had been the one spouting insults.

When Nathaniel returned from dinner, the cottage was dark. He glanced out at the back porch but wasn't surprised when he didn't see Val. He climbed the stairs. Both children were in their beds asleep, and no light glowed beneath Val's door. He didn't know what to say, but couldn't let the events from the last two days pass without speaking with her.

He knocked softly on her door. "Val?"

She didn't respond.

She had to be in there. He knew she wouldn't have left the children home alone. "I wanted to say I'm sorry. For everything." He heard movement inside her room. "Val, open the door. Can we talk?"

"Not tonight," came her muffled reply.

He didn't blame her in the least. She had to feel completely mortified by what Marielle had said, and add that to the kiss the night before…Feeling sad, Nathaniel rested his forehead against the door. "Good night, Val."

****

The next day, Val planned to be out of the house as early as possible. She texted Brandt and learned he and his friends would be spending the day at the beach by the Sea Crest Inn. The last thing she wanted was to run into Nathaniel, or his mother-in-law. Just the thought of the woman's condescending words made Val's stomach sour and her face smolder.

Mrs. Lassiter was one thing, but knowing how Val'd undoubtedly embarrassed Nathaniel—probably the entire time she'd been in Lobster Cove with her white trash clothes—felt a hundred times worse. Of course he didn't take her seriously. How could he when he was so clearly out of her league? He'd humored her all along and probably laughed at her behind her back.

His rejection after their kiss made it painfully obvious he didn't consider her to be the right kind of woman. How could she have thought otherwise?

Embarrassment and humiliating washed through her, nearly to the point of making her vomit. She breathed heavily, waiting a moment to get up the nerve to open the door. She grabbed her beach bag and purse and peeked in at Ruby and Finn before she hurried down the hall. Luckily, the kids were still asleep. She hoped Nathaniel was, too, or else maybe he was running with Seth. Stepping quietly down the stairs, she glanced toward Nathaniel's room and office, but both doors were shut.

He said her name as she laid her hand on the doorknob.

Val's heart rose into her throat. She'd only seen him for a few moments since their kiss, and those moments weren't great. She turned, but kept her gaze on the floor. "I'm sorry, I have to go. I have plans today." His feet appeared her line of sight.

"I need to talk to you."

"I don't want to talk."

"Do you plan to avoid me for the rest of the summer?" He took a step closer.

Val backed up, bumping into the door. She was acting like a petulant princess and chided herself. She was an educated independent woman, and she needed to start behaving like it. "Of course not." She raised her gaze, fighting against the emotion that seemed determined to leak out of her eyes.

"Good. I was hoping you would join us for dinner tonight." His voice was light, "Seth's coming over to grill salmon and he's bringing Melanie. Marielle and Lawrence will be here, and I thought everyone would love your cornbread and coleslaw. I know it's your day off, but I'd really appreciate it if you'd make this exception."

He sounded as if he were asking her to grab a cola at the gas station and couldn't imagine this would be distressing in the least. "Are you even kidding me right now?" She didn't know whether to scream or to cry. Her hands were shaking. Why was he doing this? Was he making fun of her? "I can't come to supper. I don't even want to be here, not after what she…" Maintaining eye contact turned out to be impossible.

"Val, I'm not letting you hide." He spoke in a serious voice. "I'm not ashamed of you. I don't care what Marielle says, and I don't want her to hurt you or make you feel like you're not welcome. I want you here tonight. We all do."

She glanced up at him and felt her heart inflate.

"You're one of us and we're in this together."

Her throat tightened as she realized what he was asking. Nathaniel wanted her to come to dinner? Did he really think Valdosta McKinley from the holler was good enough to associate with his wealthy family and friends? A bud of hope sprouted in her chest, but the feeling disappeared when she remembered Marielle's spiteful words from the day before. "But after what she said…"

"I can't believe the same woman that jumped in front of a trolley, raised her family, sold a skeptical man on abstract art, or wowed the entire town at the shooting gallery gives a second thought to the words of one haughty middle-aged woman."

Val stared at Nathaniel and her tears threatened to overflow, but for a completely different reason than before. She had no idea he felt this way. He believed in her. He was proud of her and wouldn't let Marielle tear her down. "Thank you." She opened the door. She needed to escape, either that or fall into his arms, which obviously wasn't an option.

"Seven o'clock?"

"I'll be here." Val's emotions were on a crazy rollercoaster ride. Her heart raced, her knees shook, and she didn't know whether she would end up laughing or sobbing. She'd rather find out in the privacy of her car than in front of Nathaniel.

She drove down the gravel drive, and, once out of sight of the cottage, she pulled over and leaned against the head rest. Did Nathaniel have any idea what his words accomplished? She had gone from feeling worthless to feeling like she could conquer the world. She found a pen in her purse, made a grocery list of what she'd need for the evening, and felt her smile growing.

For a moment, she daydreamed about spilling lemonade in Marielle's hair and giggled as she pulled back onto the road in better spirits than she'd felt in days. She arrived at the beach early and relaxed in the warming sun until her friends joined her. The group ate and laughed, but Val's smile had nothing to do with her company. She didn't feel bad about leaving early, even though Brandt acted as if she were breaking his heart. Instead, she looked forward to supper, to good food and friends that cared about her, but especially being with the man whose approval had come to mean more than just about anything.

Chapter Eight

Nathaniel and his children escorted Marielle and Lawrence around Lobster Cove. This time, the children were decidedly less excited about playing tourist. They'd already seen the lighthouse and statue of the Lost Fisherman. He didn't think they'd mind so much if their grandparents showed them a bit more attention, or patience. Unfortunately, Marielle and Lawrence maintained an adult pace without consideration to the tedium it must be for Ruby and Finn. He did his best to keep the children interested, but eventually resigned himself to the fact that short of a miracle, at least one of them would be whining or crying for the rest of the day.

They walked out onto the Pier 1, and Nathaniel couldn't keep his gaze from traveling to the sand beach by the Sea Crest Inn. Val had told him that was where she usually went on her day off, and he'd seen a pink swimsuit strap at her shoulder when she'd left this morning.

He didn't like the idea of Val spending the day with those people. Particularly those male people—especially when she wore what he imagined was hidden beneath her tank top and shorts. His jaw ached, and he realized he'd been clenching his teeth. He'd be glad when his life was back to normal, with his in-laws gone and Val keeping everyone happy. But was that really normal? Val would only be part of their lives for a few more weeks. The thought made him feel like his chest was caving in. Could his family return to how things were before? Could he?

On the return to the cottage, he found the front door was unlocked. *Val's back already?* He pushed it open, and the smell of baking cornbread reached him. Nathaniel was glad Val had chosen to join them. His nagging worry lessened. He knew how hard doing so must be, but he also knew she had to prove to herself she was more valuable than anything Marielle could say.

Val came from the kitchen dressed in a knee-length skirt and a T-shirt. Her hair was pulled away from her face with a band and curled softly over her shoulders and down her back. She wore a necklace he hadn't seen before.

"I was wondering when y'all would get back." She handed a bottle of Lighthouse Lager to Nathaniel and Lawrence. "Mrs. Lassiter, would you like me to pour you a glass of wine? The liquor store in Bar Harbor recommended a California Chardonnay to go with salmon."

"How lovely, thank you." Marielle spoke in a voice that sounded like a recording. Her eyes had a dazed look.

Val stood aside to allow Marielle to precede her into the kitchen. "And if you gentlemen want to wait out on the porch, you'll find a nice breeze is blowing. Seth said the salmon has just a few more minutes."

Lawrence followed his wife. He darted a questioning look at Nathaniel.

Nathaniel fought back a smile. She had certainly thrown the Lassiters off guard.

Ruby and Finn followed their grandparents into the house and pounced on Val, both talking at once.

She lifted Finn and held onto Ruby's hand, catching Nathaniel's eye just long enough to wink then joined the women in the kitchen. She introduced Melanie and Mrs. Lassiter, and poured the women's drinks then helped Ruby and Finn wash their faces and hands and listened as they described their day.

The outing was apparently much more exciting in the retelling. Nathaniel stepped through the screen door and a smile pulled at his lips. The smile grew as the full realization of what he was looking at sank in. Val had somehow managed to bring the picnic table up onto the porch from the lawn. The table was set, with a cloth and vases of fresh flowers.

Val turned sideways to squeeze by and placed a pitcher of lemonade on the table. "I figured we still have at least a few hours of daylight left, and the porch is too nice to waste." She disappeared back into the kitchen.

Nathaniel continued to stare after her. He looked at the table full of food. Alongside the cornbread, and coleslaw was a pot of baked beans, warm rolls sat in a basket and a large bowl held cut-up fruit . He leaned to catch her eye again when she came back outside, raising his eyebrows in question and tipping his head toward the table.

Val just smiled.

The gesture reminded him again how much he loved the dimples in her cheeks. He couldn't believe all the work she'd done.

"You like salmon, Val?" Seth scooped the fish from the grill onto a serving plate.

"Can't say as I've ever tried it, but the smell is delicious."

He set down the platter with a flourish. "You'll love it."

Once the food was served, Val asked Marielle about her day in Lobster Cove. She listened politely and only turned away her attention if one of the children needed her.

Nathaniel was impressed with the way Val looked Marielle in the eye and directed the conversation. He knew she fought to hide her discomfort, although he was likely the only one at the table who recognized the tension around her eyes, or the lack of light in her smile.

"I'm sure you've already heard a vacant seat will most likely be opening soon in the Massachusetts Attorney General's office," Lawrence said to Nathaniel.

Nathaniel's stomach turned with dread as one of his late wife's favorite topics was brought up. "I'd heard rumors."

Lawrence rubbed his chin. "You're more than qualified for the position, and Clara always wished to see you further your political career."

At the reminder of his wife's aspirations, Nathaniel felt a flush of heat. If his career were up to her, he'd have spent every moment campaigning and promoting himself to the right people to get ahead. And even if he were chief justice on the Supreme Court, his efforts still wouldn't have been enough

"Norah Sutherland's throwing a garden party on the twentieth, and she's assured me Myron Quinn will be there. Attending would definitely be in your best interest." Marielle raised a brow and fixed him with her direct gaze. "And, of course, you should bring Ruby and Finn."

Nathaniel had met Myron Quinn, the Attorney General for the Commonwealth of Massachusetts, on a few occasions. He had a chance of impressing the man on his own merit without pulling the "poor widower with adorable kids" card. "I can probably attend. I don't think bringing the children is necessary."

Marielle's lips pouted. "But Myron Quinn loves children. He has grandchildren of his own, you know."

The familiar expression turned his blood cold. Nathaniel didn't respond. He buttered a roll and took a bite.

Luckily, Seth asked Marielle a question and turned her attention away.

Good, he needed a minute to think. His mind turned over the possibilities. An appointment to the Attorney General's office at such a young age would put him in position to move up in the nation's legal system. *Who knew how far he could go?* He thought of the long hours he'd work, longer undoubtedly than those he was pulling now. The image of returning late at night to his cold Boston home arose in his mind.

The decision wasn't one he'd make lightly, and he wanted to talk it over with Val. As soon as he had the thought, he realized the insanity of looking for career advice from his nanny. She was a good listener, and she had nothing invested in the decision. Not that he could even call it a decision yet. He hadn't been offered the position.

After dinner, Val stood. "I hope y'all saved a bit of room for dessert. Miss Ruby, I might need some help."

Smiling, Ruby ran to her and held her hand as they

went into the kitchen.

Nathaniel watched them leave and then glanced toward Seth.

His friend smirked.

A few moments later, Val and Ruby returned. Between two hot pads, Val held a rectangular pan and Ruby carried a bowl of whipping cream.

"Where in the world did a southern girl learn to make blueberry slump?" Seth asked as he sniffed at the sweet scents coming from the pan on the table.

Val grinned. "I asked at the farmer's market and the lady selling blueberries was nice enough to share her recipe." She scooped a dumpling into a bowl and covered it in blueberry sauce then set it down next to Ruby who plopped whipped cream on top.

Once the guests had left, dishes were done, furniture returned, and kids were in bed, Nathaniel found Val on the porch listening to the waves. Calm washed over him and his muscles relaxed. *This porch truly must be magic.* "I can't believe you did all this. Putting dinner together must have taken you all day."

"Not all day." She spoke in a tired voice, leaning her head back against the chair with her eyes closed.

"But why?"

"Why what?" Val turned with her eyes squinted and her head tipped to the side.

"Why did you put so much effort into this dinner when you didn't even want to be here in the first place?" He sat in the seat next to her.

"Because I knew tonight was important to you."

Nathaniel's heart did a slow roll. He hadn't expected her answer. Knowing she'd do something so out of her comfort zone for him was astonishing.

"Thank you. Dinner, everything was perfect." He followed her lead and rested his head back with his eyes closed. He allowed his mind to wander for a moment, wondering about looking forward every day to returning home to Val's smiles and surprises. But how could he even entertain the thought? She had her heart set on Paris, and…he could take his pick of the millions of reason the relationship couldn't ever work out.

"Then the effort was completely worth it. I admit I considered wearing my bikini when I served Mrs. Lassiter's cornbread."

He could hear the smile in her voice. Nathaniel laughed. "I'd have loved to see it." He glanced at her, and when he saw her raised brow, he realized what he'd said. "I meant I'd have loved to see her face, not you in a bikini. Er, not that I wouldn't want to…"

"Aren't you supposed to be a smooth-talking attorney?" Val spoke in a teasing voice.

Nathaniel wondered if the lights were on if he'd see a blush on her cheeks. Her comment was the perfect segue way to what he'd wanted to discuss. "Did you hear what Lawrence said about the Attorney General's office?"

"Are you considering it?"

"Of course." He sat forward with his elbows on his knees. "I'm qualified, and my case record speaks for itself. That position would be a huge step in my career."

"Is it what you want?"

He couldn't see her face in the darkness, but he could imagine her expression, open, guileless, interested. *Was* it what he wanted? This sort of appointment was exactly what Clara had wanted. He'd gone along with her plans for so long, he wasn't sure exactly when her goals had become his.

"I think so. This position is what I've worked toward. I think I'm a strong candidate."

"But you aren't sure about it. Why's that?"

He wasn't sure how she could tell exactly what he was feeling but was relieved she'd seen right to the heart of the matter. "The appointment would be a huge commitment. I'd be giving up a lot of time with my kids."

Val stayed silent.

He wondered whether she was just thinking it over, or if she disapproved. Was she disappointed he was even considering the matter?

"Are you asking for my advice? Or do you just need someone to listen?"

He hadn't expected such a question. "Both, I guess."

"I know how hard growing up is with a daddy who's not there and no momma. You don't want that for Ruby and Finn, do you?"

Her words weren't a reprimand, but he felt chastised just the same. His defenses rose. "You don't think I should do it." Why did he think his nanny was the one to go to for career advice?

She twisted in the chair, holding onto his armrest and leaning toward him. "That's not true. I think you should do what's best for your career. But also for your family. If this Myron Quinn meets you, the job's yours for the taking, I guarantee. You're the hardest worker and best person I know, and if he doesn't see that, he's dumber than a bag of hammers."

"But you don't think—"

"What I think doesn't matter. Ruby and Finn will

love you either way. And I know you'd never do anything to hurt them." Silence stretched for several moments. "You don't have to take the job because other people expect you to. Your kids will be proud of you no matter what you do. And so will I."

She spoke the last sentence so quietly he strained to hear her. Her advice was the complete opposite of Clara's urgings. *Because Val didn't give me any advice at all.* She wouldn't push him either way, but trusted and supported him. Val's words warmed his chest, and his heart rolled again. "Come with me to the garden party."

"You're taking Ruby and Finn after all?"

He shifted his body to face her. "No, not the kids. You."

"I don't—" Val scratched at her nail polish.

"I want you there, Val. The event is just a few days before school starts, so the children and I will be going back to Boston anyway. We'll need to find you an apartment..." The reminder they were parting ways struck him harder than he would have imagined and made his eyes itch.

Val remained silent.

Is she dealing with the same rush of emotion? "I'm sure my friend Jason will be there, and his wife, Lisa, from the museum. His parents are old friends of the Sutherlands. You'll have a chance to meet them." He reached for her hand, feeling her jolt slightly when he held it. "Please? Your support would mean a lot."

"I appreciate you inviting me, but I have no idea how to act at something fancy like that. What would I wear?"

"You're in luck. Did I ever tell you about my sister

Rachel? Shopping's a particular talent of hers. She'll find you something."

"If you want me to, then I'll go with ya."

Nathaniel sat in the darkness and rubbed his thumb over the back of Val's hand. They had only a few weeks left in Lobster Cove, and the knowledge weighed on him. He swallowed, knowing Val was thinking the same thing as he was. The garden party was a farewell—their last time together before going their separate ways. He vowed to himself to make the night perfect. She deserved it.

****

Two weeks later, Val packed her last clothes into her suitcase and snapped it shut. Then she glanced around the room she'd grown to love, resigned to the lump that wouldn't leave her throat. She slipped her stuffed squirrel into her purse before walking across the hall to check on Ruby and Finn. Yesterday, she'd packed the kids' clothes and toys, smiling at the pictures she and Ruby had drawn and the books they'd read.

Can a heart hurt this badly?

She took the kids to the car and strapped them into their seats. Nathaniel loaded the luggage into the trunk, and Val walked through the house one more time, claiming she wanted to make sure no toys were forgotten. In truth, she hoped to fuse every inch of the cottage into her mind. She brushed her finger along the windowsill where they'd kept their shell collection, squeezed the arm of the couch they'd all cuddled in during the storm. Eventually, she ended up on the porch and couldn't hold back her tears, wiping them furiously with her fingers.

His footsteps sounded behind her.

But she didn't turn. The last thing she wanted him to see was his nanny bawling over the vacation cottage.

Nathaniel stepped closer and placed his hands on her shoulders, turning her and pulling her into his embrace.

Val clung to him, feeling utterly ridiculous, and at the same time completely content in his arms. "I'm sorry," she said, once she trusted her voice.

"The summer's been good, hasn't it?" Nathaniel laid his cheek on the top of her head and held her tighter. "I'll miss this porch most of all."

"Me, too." She pressed her face against his chest, a fresh wave of tears rushing into her eyes. She'd sat in this very place, unloading her darkest secrets, her greatest fears, been comforted and listened, and even... The memory of Nathaniel's kiss was nearly more than she could take. Her heart felt like it was being squeezed, and she gasped for air. She took a step back, releasing her grip.

"Val?"

Swallowing against her tight throat, she raised her gaze to his.

He lifted a wet strand of hair from her face, and his gaze dropped to her lips before returning to hers.

If only she could look into those blue eyes every day, be held by him every time she cried, if only...

"Daddy! Val!"

The sound of Ruby's voice broke Val's blissful bubble. She must have gotten impatient and unbuckled her carseat.

"We're on the porch, Ruby." Nathaniel's gaze didn't leave Val's face.

Val rubbed her fingers over her cheeks one more time before hurrying to meet Ruby. She glanced back and saw Nathaniel still watching her until she rounded the side of the house.

They arrived in Boston in the late afternoon and drove toward Val's new apartment. Nathaniel explained how to find the subway. "Make sure you're on the green line—outbound toward Heath. The train will drop you off right across the street from the MFA."

"Got it." Val acknowledged his instructions and kept her gaze directed out the window, memorizing her way through the narrow, curving streets and brown brick buildings that were all smashed together and looked the same.

Nathaniel drove through the neighborhood, showing her the closest grocery store, and finally stopped in front of the apartment building, double checking the address. Cars lined both sides of the street, and so he left the car idling as they got out. He lifted her suitcase from the trunk. "You sure the manager is meeting you?"

Val nodded as she took a hold of the handle, knowing she didn't dare raise her gaze to his face. "He just texted me."

Nathaniel looked at the building, and then back, clearing his throat. "You still planning on tomorrow night?"

"If you still want me."

He took her hand, squeezing it. "I'll bring Rachel over in the morning—nine o'clock. Will that work?"

"Thanks for doing that." She tried to smile but the gesture fell flat as she looked through the back window where Ruby and Finn slept in their seats. Who would feed them supper tonight? Pour extra bubbles in Finn's bath? Put a sleeping spell on Ruby? "Tell them good-bye for me. And tell them…" Her throat tightened, and she couldn't make her voice finish the sentence.

"I'll tell them."

****

Nathaniel drove through the familiar streets to Beacon Hill, but the trip didn't feel like he was going *home*. The word should invoke a feeling of warmth, happiness, and love. While his house was beautiful, set in one of the most desirable neighborhoods in the country, he didn't consider it to be any of these things.

His mind kept returning to Val. Of course it did, because his brain was determined to torture him. The image of her waving from the front of the apartment building with her old orange suitcase while she faked a smile brought an ache to the back of his throat.

How would he explain to Ruby and Finn Val wasn't living with them anymore? How could he explain it to himself? His feelings for her were pretty obvious by now. He was in love with her. Of course, Seth had been right.

And he thought Val may love him too. Did she? His breath caught at the memory of their kiss, the way she'd looked at him this morning when he'd held her as she cried. Her unrestrained smile and dimpled cheeks, the laughter that bubbled up from her toes, and the simple moments like sitting in silence on the porch or sharing a look when one of the kids said something funny. How would he live without these things? And why should he? Why wasn't he driving back to that apartment, breaking down her door, and kissing her senseless?

His fingers tightened on the steering wheel. He knew exactly why. *Paris*. Val had a dream, and if he saddled her with two kids and a husband who worked twelve to fourteen hours a day in a city she didn't know, she'd come to resent him for taking away the dream. Not to mention, Boston High Society would eat her alive. Marielle was mild compared to how cruel people could be to someone who didn't fit in.

Val deserved a chance at an exciting life. She was smart, outgoing, and she'd make friends wherever she went. And she should to find her way, rather than being tied down and following his career instead of her own.

This was the right thing. The decision hurt, but they both knew parting was for the best, and in time the pain would ease.

Tomorrow, Rachel would find Val a dress. Then Val and he would be together one last time at the garden party. He'd make sure she knew how special she was, how beautiful.

He had built up this evening in his mind, not understanding himself why it had become so important. Maybe because the event represented the ending of something that had meant a lot to them both. Maybe he wanted to give Val an experience to remember him by. Maybe his reasoning wasn't as altruistic as he'd led himself to believe. He selfishly wanted Val at the garden party, whether to prove something to herself, to Marielle, or just because she was the one he wanted beside him at an event that could change his life. Whatever the reason, the night would be special. He'd make sure of it. The last gift he'd give Val would be to let her go and follow her dreams.

He would have never imagined making such a

decision would be physically painful.

Half an hour later, he woke up Ruby when they reached the parking garage. "Come on, honey. I need you to walk so I can carry Finn."

She rubbed her eyes and looked at the front passenger seat. "Where's Val?"

Nathaniel's chest was tight. "Remember, Val has her own house now, and we're back here at ours."

Ruby crossed her arms. "I don't want to be at our house. I want to be in Maine with Val."

He unbuckled Finn, lifted the boy from his car seat then walked to the other side of the car, and opened Ruby's door. "Come on inside, sweetheart. I bet Mrs. Kimball has dinner all ready."

She climbed out of the car but stood next to it instead of walking to their house. "I don't like it in Boston."

Nathaniel sighed. He didn't have the patience for one of Ruby's tantrums and wished he knew how to diffuse it before it started. He shifted Finn onto his shoulder and reached to take Ruby's hand, leading her out of the parking garage and down the lamp-lit street. "Of course you like it here, Ruby. Your toys are here, and your friends.

"No, I don't. I don't want to be here." She pulled her hand from his and stood on the sidewalk, glaring at their front door.

Nathaniel sighed. "Ruby, honey. We're all tired. You'll feel happier in the morning. Just come on inside, and we'll eat dinner and—"

"You're not a daddy in Boston." Ruby stomped her foot and her curls bounced. "We never see you here. You're always at work or on the phone. I want to go back to Maine." Her lower lip quivered and her shoulders shook.

Her words hit Nathaniel so hard that he sucked in a heavy breath. Coldness spread from his core. He had no idea his daughter felt this strongly. He hurried up the steps and unlocked the front door, handing Finn to the housekeeper and then knelt on the brick sidewalk next to Ruby. "I'll still be your daddy whether we're in Boston or Maine."

She shook her head, covering her face with her hands.

Nathaniel lifted her into his arms and carried her into the house. He sat on a chair in the living room and set her on his lap, holding her tightly as he hushed her cries.

Ruby wrapped her arms around his neck and sobbed onto his shoulder.

If Clara were here, she'd tell him one day Ruby would appreciate all the hard work and sacrifice he made for the family.

He tried to think of what Val would say. He felt the side of his mouth lift and let out a sigh. Val would support him in anything he did, picking up the slack where his parenting skills fell short. He rubbed circles on her back and kissed the top of her head. The career goals he'd had since college didn't hold the same appeal as they once did. But was he just being sentimental? Inside, he felt the rift between his work goals and his family widening. With a sinking feeling, he worried choosing one would mean giving up the other.

****

The next morning, Nathaniel met Rachel in front of

Val's apartment building.

She didn't even wait for him to get out of his car before she bombarded him with questions. "Why can't this woman find a dress herself?"

"Listen, I explained this before. She's from out of town, and she needs something for tonight."

She flipped her hair over her shoulder. "Where did you meet her? Are you dating?"

He stepped out of the car, closed the door behind him, and folded his arms across his chest. "We're not dating. Val's going to Europe in a few months, and I'm taking her to the Sutherland's garden party tonight. Why is this so difficult to understand?"

"Because a request like this is so out of character for you."

He ignored her for the few minutes needed to enter the building and climb the stairs in the narrow hallway. Nathaniel knocked on Val's apartment door and shushed his sister one more time. "Be gentle with her, she's not used to this kind of thing."

She lifted her palms. "What kind of thing? Shopping?"

Val opened the door and when she saw Rachel, she lowered her gaze and then raised it again with a shy smile. She stepped back. "Come on in."

Nathaniel had never seen the expression on Val's face and realized how nervous she must be. He introduced the women and glanced around the space, relieved the apartment appeared nicely furnished. He noticed the stuffed squirrel sat on a shelf in the living room.

Val looked at the shelf, too, and her cheeks turned pink. "How did Ruby and Finn do last night?"

"Good." He didn't tell her about Ruby's tears or Finn's tantrum when Val didn't prepare his breakfast. "They did well." He thought she looked as if she'd ask more, and he was grateful when his sister interrupted.

"Are you ready to go?" Rachel took a step back toward the door.

Val picked up her purse from where it hung on the back of a kitchen chair.

When Rachel saw it, she lowered her chin. "First order of business. New purse, hold the pink fur."

Nathaniel cleared his throat.

Val frowned as she glanced at her purse and then back to Rachel.

He studied Val's face and let out a breath when her expression relaxed.

Rachel nodded and smiled. "We'll have fun today, Val. And don't worry, big brother, I'll have her home in time for the ball."

Seeing Val's expression was still strained, Nathaniel gave an encouraging smile, hoping to set her at ease. She was obviously nervous about spending the day with a stranger.

They entered the hallway, and she closed the door behind them, turning the knob to make sure it locked.

Once they reached the sidewalk in front of the building, Nathaniel opened the door for Val to get into Rachel's car and shot a look at his sister. She held up her hands, widening her eyes in a look he could clearly read as telling him to "cool it."

He stuffed his hands in his pockets and watched as they pulled away, then drove to work, knowing he couldn't concentrate on anything today while he wondered how Val was doing, what she looked like in her dress, and how could he say good bye to her tonight.

Chapter Nine

Val shifted in her seat, unsure what to say to Nathaniel's sister. Rachel was tall, slender, elegant, sophisticated...The complete opposite of Val. She guessed the dark-haired woman was a few years younger than Nathaniel. Confident and beautiful.

Val stared out the window as the city went by, hoping she didn't look like a wide-eyed country hick, but she couldn't help it. Boston was amazing. The city was made up of uniform brick buildings with different colored doors, varying doorframes, awnings, and flowers in window boxes to distinguish them from one another. They passed old-looking churches and historic-looking buildings. Quaint streetlamps and brick sidewalks contrasted with neon signs hanging in windows.

Rachel pulled onto Newbury Street and found a parking spot. She put the car into gear and turned it off.

Val reached for the door handle.

"We have a few minutes before anything opens." Rachel fished in her purse and offered a pack of gum to Val, then tore a piece in half, and chewed. "That's enough time for you to tell me what's really going on with you and my brother."

Val had just popped the stick in her mouth. "I don't know what you mean," she said around the wad of gum.

She lowered her eyes to half-mast and tipped her

head. "I mean, why is Nathaniel so worried about finding a dress for a woman I've never heard of until a few days ago? How do you even know him?"

"I was his nanny this summer. In Lobster Cove." Rachel's plucked brows rose so high Val thought they would disappear into her hair line.

"His nanny? He's taking his *nanny* to a garden party at the Sutherlands?"

Val rubbed her arm. Rachel was definitely less than impressed. "I know, the arrangement sounds weird."

"Not just weird. He's acting crazy." She pushed her hair over her shoulder. "You know he chewed out one of your neighbors who held open the entry door, instead of letting it lock and waiting for you to buzz us in."

Val was startled and confused. She had no idea what she should say. *What would make Nathaniel so upset that he got after a person for being friendly?*

Rachel flipped her hand to the side. "And then there's the whole, 'help my friend find a pretty dress.' Honestly, I don't know what to think. I've never seen him act this way."

"He must think I need extra help with my East Coast fashion sense." Val waved her hand, indicating her Daisy Duke cut-offs and tank top. Her face heated. "I don't want to embarrass him at the garden party."

Rachel squinted her eyes as she studied Val.

Under the blue-eyed gaze, Val felt like a bug under a microscope and tried not to squirm.

"You're in love with him."

Tears sprang into Val's eyes, and she blinked them away. She realized she hadn't even admitted the truth to herself, and hearing the words caught her so off guard she didn't have a chance to school her expression. "How pathetic, right? The nanny that's in love with her boss. Please don't tell him."

"Honey, why do you think he's doing all this? Do you really think he'd give me his credit card and send his nanny on a shopping spree unless he felt the same? I mean, I love my brother, but he just plain isn't that thoughtful. I guarantee his assistant's sent me flowers on my birthday for the last five years. He probably doesn't even know what date it is." She gave a smirk and small shrug.

Val folded the gum wrapper, creasing it with her nails. Her heart was pounding as her mind spun. Was Rachel right? Did Nathaniel love her? She turned away and looked at the buildings outside the car window, hoping to keep Rachel from seeing the turmoil inside her. She attempted an off-handed tone as she spoke. "Maybe his wife sent them?"

"Ha! Clara? Not in a million years. That woman was the worst thing to happen to my brother." Her lip curled in a sneer. "And to the world."

Val sucked in a breath. Rachel seemed so collected. "You didn't like her?"

"Honey, let's put it this way...if Clara was on fire and I had a cup of water, I'd drink it."

Val laughed. She was starting to like Nathaniel's sister.

"She hated me." Rachel's teeth showed as she talked. "And the feeling was completely mutual."

Based on Rachel's expression, Val wouldn't have been surprised if she'd spit or growled while she talked about Clara. "Why?"

"The harpy tore down my brother every chance she

got—until he was hardly recognizable as the same kid I grew up with." Rachel's eyes squinted, and her brows pulled together in a scowl. Her face flushed a rosy hue. "And no matter how terribly he was treated, he still did everything he could to make her happy. Finally I'd had enough, and I told her so."

"What happened?" Val struggled inside between the need to hear about Nathaniel, and knowing his past was none of her business. The more she heard about his marriage, the sadder she felt.

"Well, let's just say I didn't get invited for Christmas dinner." Rachel shrugged.

Val thought his sister faked like the slight hadn't bothered her, but her feelings had certainly been hurt.

"I could see choosing between the two of us was getting too hard for Nathaniel, and, anyway…after that I didn't see him very often." Rachel pulled her keys out of the ignition and dropped them into her purse. "That woman took away my only family." She opened the car door and stepped out.

Val followed suit. "I'm sorry," she said when she joined Rachel on the sidewalk. "Not having your family nearby hurts." They walked past several shops. Rachel apparently knew just where she was going.

"And where's your family, Val?"

"West Virginia."

"Ah, so that's why you speak all Southern and sultry like Scarlett O'Hara."

Rachel's voice sounded lighter, and Val felt relieved she wasn't still talking about Clara. "Y'all might call it sultry, but I don't think my accent always gives a good first impression."

Rachel pulled open the glass door of a shop and

ushered Val inside. "Well, honey, that's where I come in. Your first impression tonight will knock everyone's socks off. That brother of mine won't know what hit him."

Val looked around when they entered the shop and was tempted to hurry back outside. The shop was cramped, but the clothing on display was sophisticated and beautiful, making her feel like a toad who'd hopped into a frog pond.

The saleslady greeted Rachel by name and when she heard what they were looking for, she smiled and showed Val to a dressing room.

Val stepped out of her clothes and slid on gown after gown, zipping and tying and buttoning until she thought she must have tried on every outfit in the shop.

But the saleslady and Rachel both kept bringing more. Rachel insisted she try on slacks and blouses in addition to formal gowns.

Val argued, but Rachel said she was just following orders.

After more than an hour, Val slipped on a champagne-colored pleated gown with a gold belt. Looking into the mirror, she couldn't believe the elegant looking person was really Valdosta McKinley from the holler. She lifted the floor-length skirt and walked out of the dressing room.

"That's the one." Rachel turned Val by the shoulders to look in the half-circle of mirrors. "You look absolutely amazing." She lifted the shoulder seams and checked the waist. "And it fits perfectly, even better—no alterations." She tapped a finger on her chin. "I think maybe pearls, and you'll need to wear your hair down…"

"I love it." Val held out the skirt and swished it back and forth. She felt beautiful and couldn't wait to see Nathaniel's face when he saw her in the gown. But when she turned over the tag, she couldn't stop her fingers from flying to her lips, and she gasped. "Oh. Is that the price? I had no idea the dress would cost this much. I couldn't possibly."

Rachel put her hands on her hips. "Val, I can't face Nathaniel if I don't do exactly what he asked. Now hurry and change out of the gown. We still need to find shoes and stop at the spa. And of course, have lunch."

They dropped the gown off at the car, along with a few other items Rachel had purchased while Val changed. At the day spa, Rachel ordered a haircut, mani/pedi, and facial for both of them. A make-up artist worked on Val's face.

Rachel waved away Val's concern about the amount of money they were spending. "Val, take up your complaints with the boss. I'm just fulfilling my assignment."

They returned home late in the afternoon. Rachel helped Val carry the packages and bags to her apartment. In addition to her clothing for tonight, Val had a few nice outfits, shoes, and scarves Rachel told her were exactly the thing an art museum employee would wear.

Noting the time, Val freshened up then changed into her dress and stepped into her new shoes.

Rachel hung the remaining clothes in the closet. Chattering away as she fussed with the fit, she helped Val attach her necklace and smoothed down her hair.

Val studied her appearance in the bathroom mirror. She couldn't believe her new chic look with her hair cut and straightened. And the dress was spectacular.

The buzzer rang.

Val answered it, heart racing now that Nathaniel was here and on his way upstairs.

"Don't worry. He won't be able to keep his eyes off you."

I hope not. Val hugged Rachel. "Thank you. I could never have done this myself." She'd loved spending the day with Rachel, and thought how much she'd enjoyed having a friend in the city. Rachel had turned out to be so different than Val's first impression.

"Careful, don't wrinkle your dress." Rachel held her at arm's length and smiled. "And today was my pleasure, Val." She opened the door.

Nathaniel entered carrying a vase of multi-colored roses. He wore a tuxedo that fit him perfectly and stood straight and confident. His eyes widened when he saw Val.

Val clasped her hands so he wouldn't see them shaking.

He thrust the flowers at his sister, still holding Val's gaze. "Shall we?" The side of his mouth lifted in a smile.

Val hadn't realized how tightly she'd been holding her shoulders until she released them. She had no reason to be nervous. Nathaniel's familiar smile had somehow calmed her nerves and set them tingling at the same time. She would never tire of the sensation.

"That's my cue to leave." Rachel set the vase on the table, grabbed her bag, and wiggled her fingers in a wave as she stepped around her brother. She winked at Val before closing the door behind her.

"I just need my purse." Val hurried into her

bedroom and grabbed the clutch Rachel selected to match her dress, and then returned to the living room.

"You look beautiful, Val." Nathaniel made a twirling motion with his finger, smiling as Val turned in a circle. "How did you and Rachel get along?"

"We had a fabulous day. Thanks for arranging everything and for the dress, and..." She glanced toward her bedroom where hundreds of dollars' worth of clothing hung in her closet. "Why did you do all this? You didn't need to have Rachel buy me clothes."

Nathaniel lifted a shoulder and tipped his head toward it. "You're starting a new job on Monday, and I just wanted you to—"

"To look decent for your friend?" Val didn't mean for her words to sound ungrateful, but she felt insecure about her clothing already, and she hated the idea that he was ashamed of her just like Bo Callaway had been. Was Nathaniel so afraid she'd humiliate him, he didn't mind spending all that money to make sure she didn't show up looking like a redneck from the holler?

He lifted up his chin. "How you look doesn't matter as much as how you feel. I want you to feel confident on Monday."

Val felt her insides squirm. She still felt guilty and thought she could probably return the clothes. "But I have so much money from working all summer. I can buy clothes. I can pay you back for all this. You don't have to—"

"Your money won't last as long as you think, especially in Europe. Consider them a thank you for all you did for me and the kids."

Val blinked. Nobody had ever done anything so nice before, and she wasn't sure how to respond. She was so touched he would look out for her and care about how she felt at her new job. Was Rachel right about Nathaniel? Did he love her like she loved him? She could easily give up Paris if he'd only ask. Would tonight be the beginning of something? Or would it be the end?

He offered his arm, smiling.

"Thank you, Nathaniel. I can't tell you what it means." She slid her hand into the crook of his elbow and allowed him to lead her out to his car.

Nathaniel drove through the city and into a neighborhood with Colonial-style homes and large trees. He pulled through the high gates of a walled estate and drove to the front of the Sutherland's house.

Val thought it looked more like a hotel or a mortuary. The building was made of brick. White columns stood on either side of the front entry, supporting a small deck with a wrought-iron railing.

He told her the house was over two hundred and fifty years old, one of the oldest mansions in the country.

"It's beautiful." Val was grateful Rachel had helped her today. She may feel out of place, but she knew she didn't look it.

He smiled and raised a brow. "Wait until you see the grounds."

A valet opened her door and held Val's hand as she climbed out of the car.

Nathaniel joined her at the entry. "You really are beautiful, you know?" He slid his fingers through the ends of her hair that was now nearly a foot shorter, and barely reached her shoulders. The side of his mouth pulled into his crooked smile, and he took her hand.

Val's nervousness vanished, and all she noticed was Nathaniel's hand and the way it made her heart trip when it clasped hers. How could something as simple as holding hands make her breathless? She hoped he wouldn't release it when they encountered more guests.

They walked through the doors and into an entry foyer. A large chandelier hung from the ceiling, and a glass sculpture sat on a pedestal in the center of the hall.

Val slowed as they passed the sculpture.

Nathaniel continued to hold her hand as they walked slowly around it.

"It's perfect." Val made a curling motion with her fingers. "See how the swirls intertwine? It's seemingly random, but each is placed in the exact right spot. The glass looks as if it's moving, dancing. And the colors set the perfect mood with lavenders and aqua. I think it represents the unpredictability, and yet calmness, of the sea. " She continued to admire the piece, amazed the Sutherlands had something this remarkable sitting in their front room.

"You must be Val." A woman spoke from behind her.

Val hadn't even noticed her approach, she'd been so intent upon the sculpture. She was accompanied by a man, and Val didn't recognize either of them. How had the woman known her name?

Nathaniel released her hand to shake with the man. "Jason, Lisa, we were hoping you'd be here. I'd like you to meet Valdosta McKinley. Val, this is Jason and Lisa Krauss. Lisa's your new boss."

"Pleased to meet you." Val was glad she looked so sophisticated. She held out her hand. Lisa's dark hair was cut into a short bob, longer on one side, and her colorful dress was asymmetrical. Val should have known by her trendy appearance she was an assistant curator at an art museum.

She shook Val's hand and pointed toward the table. "The sculpture's amazing, isn't it?"

Val nodded. "I've never seen anything like it.

Lisa put her hand to the side of her mouth and leaned close to whisper, "We have much better pieces at the MFA."

She put on an expression that back home would be called "hoity-toity," but smiled to let Val know she was teasing.

Val liked her immediately.

"I heard you describe this one. You really know what you're talking about." Her eyes narrowed as she glanced at Nathaniel and then back to Val, looking her up and down. "I have to say, you're not what I expected at all."

Val wondered what Lisa meant. Nathaniel had called his friend and secured the job the day he'd met Val. Just thinking about that day—her teased hair, globs of makeup, torn skirt…She couldn't imagine what Nathaniel had to say to convince his friend to hire her. She hoped Lisa wouldn't regret it.

Nathaniel seemed relaxed as he talked with Jason Krauss, and Val remembered he'd mentioned Jason was a college buddy. She was glad to see him smile as they spoke about mutual friends, baseball, and lawyer-y things, and she was relieved Lisa was friendly, even though her manner was abrupt. Val was realizing New Englanders were much more direct than she was used to. Lisa seemed like someone Val would enjoy working for.

Lisa showed Val a few of the paintings in the Sutherland's downstairs rooms, asking questions, and listening with her head tipped to the side to Val's assessment of the pieces.

Nathaniel opened a patio door and the soft sounds of a string quartet greeted them as they walked outside to join the party.

Val shrunk back as she saw the number of elegant people gathered.

Again, Nathaniel took her hand, squeezing it as they walked with the Krausses toward a vacant table covered in a long white tablecloth. He pulled out a chair for Val to sit, and then joined her.

Lisa sat on her other side with her husband.

Val couldn't believe how beautiful the Sutherlands' yard was. Manicured hedges lined paths leading beneath wrought-iron arches from one garden to the next. Each was a showcase of flowers and color. A pool was on one side of the patio with glowing glass orbs floating on the water. Pots and jars of plants ringed the patio and on the tables. A stream flowed down the other side of the yard, and the sound of trickling water reminded Val for a moment of the creek that flowed near her daddy's trailer. She closed her eyes and listened until Lisa spoke again.

"Nathaniel told me something about you moving to Europe in a few months?"

"I'm applying for an internship in Paris. That's why I wanted some experience in—"

"At *L'Académie de l'Art Magnifique*? Lisa leaned forward and pressed her hands together. Seeing Val's nod, she continued. "That's where I studied. I'll write you a glowing recommendation. Madame Bissette, the headmistress, is a good friend of mine."

"That would be wonderful." Val hoped her expression showed the excitement she didn't feel. Paris no longer held the same appeal, and she almost dreaded the idea of leaving, especially after what Rachel had said. She glanced at Nathaniel.

He studied her.

She wondered what he was thinking. Could he tell what was going on in her mind? Did he feel the same?

A server brought hors d'oeuvres and drinks, and Val was grateful Nathaniel and Jason changed the topic to the Red Sox.

Jason draped his arm across the back of his wife's chair, and Nathaniel held onto Val's hand as the men argued about sports.

Val watched the people at the party. She'd never seen such beautiful dresses or so much sparkling jewelry. Elegant people clustered around holding goblets of champagne. The scene reminded Val of a red-carpet event on T.V.

"You know…" Jason leaned in toward Nathaniel, lowering his voice. "Myron Quinn's here tonight." He darted his gaze in the direction of a man with thick gray hair walking between the tables.

Nathaniel looked in Myron's direction and then back at Jason. "I'd heard he might be."

Jason raised his brows. "Did you also hear an opening will be available soon in the Attorney General's office?"

Nathaniel dipped his chin in a nod.

Val saw the edges of his eyes squint, a gesture she recognized as nervousness, but he lowered his brows.

"You've got to be one of the top on his list." Jason

chewed his lip.

Nathaniel didn't comment, but he looked back toward Myron Quinn.

A moment later, Jason and Lisa excused themselves when they saw Jason's parents.

"See you Monday morning, Val." Lisa waved and took her husband's hand.

Nathaniel leaned close to speak in her ear. "I don't think you could have impressed her more if you'd whipped out an easel and painted a masterpiece."

His closeness and his breath on her cheek made Val shiver. She squeezed his hand.

Nathaniel stood.

Val turned to see a woman approaching them.

Nathaniel took the woman's hands and pecked a kiss on her cheek, and then turned. "Val, I'd like you to meet Mrs. Sutherland. Norah, this is my friend, Valdosta McKinley."

Norah tipped back her head and narrowed her eyes as she looked at Val.

"How do you do?" Val shook her hands and tried not to fidget beneath the woman's scrutiny. "Your place is beautiful."

"Marielle's told me about you, Val. And what an interesting choice of companions, Nathaniel. Not many men would bring their nanny."

Val cringed back at the woman's words. She was horrified her presence would cause Nathaniel any awkwardness.

Nathaniel held her hand tighter, pulling her to his side. "Actually, Val works at the Museum of Fine Arts."

The sides of Norah's mouth turned down, creating

large wrinkles on her cheeks and neck and demonstrating perfectly why middle-aged women shouldn't make that particular expression. "How nice." She turned, her motion dismissing Val, and spoke exclusively to Nathaniel. "And did you know Myron Quinn is here?"

"Yes, I saw him earlier."

"You'll certainly want to speak with him before the night is over." Norah raised a brow in a knowing look. She nodded once before she excused herself.

Val and Nathaniel exchanged a glance as Norah Sutherland walked away.

He rolled his eyes. "That could have been much worse. How about a walk around the gardens before it's too dark to appreciate them?" Nathaniel led her away from the tables, down a shrub-lined path.

Each garden was more magnificent than the last. Val wondered if she'd love them quite as much if Nathaniel were not holding her hand, walking next to her in a striking tuxedo. She saw women glance at him, and she felt proud he would choose to bring her to this event, and be seen so publicly with her.

Nathaniel led her to a wrought-iron bench beneath a large tree next to the brook.

She brushed her hand over the bench to make sure nothing would get on her dress before sitting next to him. The setting couldn't have been more amazing if she'd planned it. The sun neared the horizon, and lights came on all around. The sky glowed with a golden tint, and a soft breeze carrying the fragrance of hundreds of flowers floated around them. Val sighed. "I can't imagine any place more perfect."

He raised her hand, brushing his lips across her

knuckles. "I can't imagine any company more perfect."

The gesture sent waves of tingles up her arm. "Actually, I think I love the porch at Couthy Cottage better."

Nathaniel twisted toward her and rested his arm across the back of the bench. "That old place?" He shook his head, but then he winked.

Val pretended to swat him. "Yes, that old place. It's special."

His eyes lost their playfulness. "I think we can credit the memories more than the location." He brushed his hand up her arm, bringing it to rest on her shoulder.

"I wish—" Val began but couldn't finish. Her thoughts were muddled as she lost herself in his eyes.

Nathaniel's gaze held hers. "What do you wish, Val?" His voice was raspy and deep as he bent closer, his mouth hovering over hers. "Tell me what you wish," he whispered against her lips.

Val's heartbeat sounded in her ears. How could she tell him what she truly wished? That she loved him and his kids and wanted to be with them. "I wish summer wasn't over." She rested her hand on his chest, feeling his heart beat as he touched his lips to hers again, tentatively, as if he were waiting. She slid her hand to the back of his head, and in an instant, his lips moved against hers and the kiss changed from tender to urgent.

Val's heart pummeled against her ribs as Nathaniel pulled her closer. His hands were cupped beneath her jaw, his fingers threaded in her hair. A wave of fire moved from her lips, skittering over her skin. When their lips separated, they each breathed heavily. He rested his forehead on hers, and she didn't want to open her eyes. Didn't want to hear the music or the brook or the wisps of distant conversations or to feel the bench poking awkwardly against her hip. She didn't want to wake up from her dream and have the perfect moment end.

Nathaniel moved away and stood, pulling her up. "Think we should walk some more?"

Val worried her knees wouldn't support her, but she nodded.

They strolled beneath arches and through the gardens until he led her back to the patio area.

She wondered what he was thinking. Was he sorry he'd kissed her again? He didn't seem like he was but how could she tell? He hadn't kept kissing her which in itself wasn't a good sign.

They walked back toward the patio. In the darkness, the conversations seemed louder, whether the increase in volume was just a trick of the mind, or whether the night and champagne had freed inhibitions, Val didn't know. She scooted closer to Nathaniel, but she felt him stiffen. She glanced at his face and then followed his gaze to Myron Quinn.

Myron lifted his chin as he approached. "Nathaniel Cavanaugh, just the person I've been looking for."

"Good evening, Mr. Quinn. May I introduce my friend, Valdosta McKinley?"

"A pleasure." Myron shook Val's hand." Enjoying the evening, Miss McKinley?"

She realized this man was the reason for Nathaniel's tension. "It's been lovely."

"I hope you don't mind if I take Nathaniel away to speak privately for a moment?"

"Course not. Y'all take your time. I'll be just fine."

She squeezed Nathaniel's hand, wishing him luck.

He squeezed it back before releasing her and walking with Myron Quinn toward the house.

Val wandered around the party. She tried a few hors d'oeuvres and scanned the group for Lisa and Jason, hoping to join someone who she knew. Finally, she sat at a table and watched people moving among the different groups, laughing and talking. She overheard bits of conversation and the more she listened, the more she realized this high society would never feel comfortable. She'd be much more at home if the band had a fiddle and the gardens had a mud pit. Her gaze moved over the gathering, and one woman caught her eye. Val's stomach sank.

Marielle Lassiter approached, her long blue gown swishing as she walked.

Val stood and tried to smile calmly. "Hello, Mrs. Lassiter. Y'all look beautiful tonight."

Marielle didn't acknowledge Val's greeting. "I didn't believe it when Norah told me. But it's true. He brought his *nanny* to one of the most important events of the year."

Val was surprised by the offensive tone in the woman's voice. "Actually, ma'am, I'm not working for Mr. Cavanaugh anymo—"

"I don't know what Nathaniel's thinking. Obviously, he's lonely and letting his hormones call the shots. He's just not thinking straight since Clara died." She tapped her finger on the diamond pendant at her throat, shaking her head.

"Mrs. Lassiter, nothing inappropriate is happening. Nathaniel brought me tonight as a friend."

Marielle's eyes narrowed at the use of his first

name.

Without Nathaniel next to her, any bit of self-confidence Val possessed trickled away under the woman's glare. She looked down and picked at her nail polish.

"Listen, *Val.*"

The sarcastic tone Marielle used made Val want to shrink.

"We both know you don't belong here. Are you so selfish you'd ruin his career?" She leaned closer.

Val was reminded of a mad possum hissing and baring its teeth when it's cornered. "I don't understand what you mean. Course I don't want to ruin Nathaniel's career." How could her presence at a garden party affect his career?

"Let me put it as gently as possible. People talk. The two of you have been living together for months." She held up a hand against Val's protest. "Whether anything untoward has occurred or not, you're still living in the same house. With his *children*." Marielle paused.

Val considered what she'd said, but she could not understand what Marielle meant.

"He arrives with you here tonight, on the cusp of his political career. All that's needed to ruin him is a few pictures of you in your "summer" attire, and the scandal would put a permanent blight on his reputation."

A surge of heat exploded in Val's face. Her words couldn't be true. But Val thought of news stories of politicians, movie stars, sports players, and knew Marielle was right. All these men with their pictures on magazine covers with headlines telling the world what scumbags they were. Nobody took the time to check facts. People just wanted a story, and even more, they wanted a scandal. She couldn't let Nathaniel be smeared like that. Val's stomach clenched into a tight knot. "I didn't realize…"

"Well now you do." Marielle dipped her head in a quick nod and left to rejoin a group of women.

Val's unease grew as she gazed around the garden party. Were all these people speaking about Nathaniel? Did they think he was anything less than the perfect person for the Attorney General's office? The thought that she could ruin everything made her panicky and light headed. She needed to leave. They hadn't spoken to many people. Maybe if they left now, people wouldn't wonder who she was or why they were together. She moved to another chair that was further shadowed, hoping nobody would notice her, and then after tapping her toes and chewing on her nails, she walked down the path deeper into the gardens where hardly any guests had wandered.

Moments later, she heard footsteps and turned quickly.

"There you are. I've been looking everywhere for you." Nathaniel walked up the path to join her.

Val was nearly ready to tear out her hair. She pushed away her anxiety, however, when she saw the expression on his face.

"The job's mine if I want it." He leaned toward her.

His smile was excited. And nervous. Val shifted away, avoiding his embrace. "I knew you could do it. They'll be lucky to have you." She looked around at the people, wondering if any were watching them.

Nathaniel cocked his head to the side, studying her face. "Are you okay? Did something happen?"

"I'm great. I'm so proud of you, and...I think we should leave."

Nathaniel straightened. "Leave?"

"It's getting late, and you don't want to be away from the kids too long, and—"

"Val, what's wrong?" He touched her shoulder.

"I'm just feeling tired. It's been a long day. I still need to get groceries tomorrow—"

He took her arm. "What happened?"

"Nothing. I just want to leave." Val's desperation made her voice sharper than she'd intended. But maybe that way he wouldn't question her anymore.

Nathaniel flinched and released his hold. "All right."

"We did it, right?" she said.

He squinted. "Did we?"

"You got your dream job, and Paris looks like a sure thing. We both got what we wanted." The words tasted bitter in her mouth.

"I guess we did."

The air between them thickened as they walked back through the house and retrieved the car. Val tried to think of something to say, but anything that came to mind was either flippant and inconsequential or too painful for their last moments. Because that's what this was. Their last time together.

Earlier, she'd thought maybe this night was a beginning for them. She was no longer his nanny but a woman living in his town, someone he might want to...But a relationship just couldn't be. They couldn't be. Tonight wasn't a beginning, but the ending. Val took in a jerky breath, determined not to cry in front of him again. Not after he'd made this night so wonderful. She wouldn't have his last memory of their time together ruined by her tears.

When they arrived at her apartment, she smiled, but she couldn't manage to push out the torrent of words blocked at the back of her throat. She wanted to tell him she loved him, that she needed him, that she'd do anything to be with him if they could find a way.

They walked silently to her door, and Val unlocked it, pushing it ajar before turning, intending to think of something cheerful to say, but she couldn't.

Gaze locked on hers, he took her hand and then the other, pulling her closer and then cradled her cheeks in his palms.

Val squeezed her eyes shut to force back the tears that surged forward.

Nathaniel lowered his mouth to hers, but this kiss wasn't like the others. The kiss wasn't a tentative first kiss or an urgent hungry kiss. He kissed her slowly, sadly. A final kiss, full of sorrow and longing.

He pulled away, and Val felt like something was ripped from her. She drew in a breath as she opened her eyes and met his gaze. Her pulse raced.

"Good bye Val." He released her face and stepped back.

She wrapped her arms around her stomach, hoping to keep the ache contained and stumbled into her apartment, closing the door and leaning against it. She slid down, putting her head on her knees, and sobbed as her heart shattered into small bits.

Chapter Ten

As he rode in the town car, Nathaniel checked his email. He glanced up at the Boston Garden, then back down as he scrolled through tomorrow's schedule and then, out of habit, returned the phone to his pocket before the lock screen appeared. He'd been jarred enough times by the picture of his family and Val at the lighthouse that he'd made it a habit to look away before the image came up. He couldn't quite make himself change it.

The interim seemed like another lifetime since he'd returned from Maine, even though only six weeks had passed. Seeing the picture and remembering the time spent with his family and Val produced an emptiness he was completely unable to deal with. Things would slow at the State Attorney General's office around the holidays, and then he'd make it up to his kids. And as for Val. He didn't even let himself think about her anymore. Not when just seeing her picture on his phone made his chest ache.

He looked up and realized the car had stopped at his destination. He'd had no idea his new job would require him to attend so many receptions and fundraisers. He tried to think of the last evening he'd spent at home and then pushed away the twist of guilt at the memory of Ruby's words. *You're not a daddy in Boston.* Besides, he couldn't miss this event. Even though he'd technically been working at the Attorney General's office for a few weeks, tonight, he'd be officially introduced by Myron as the newest member of his staff.

After exiting the car, he crossed the sidewalk then rode the elevator to the ballroom on the top floor. He brushed a hand over the lapels of his tuxedo and lifted a glass of champagne from a tray offered by a server. He scanned the room and a wave of nervousness rolled over his skin as he saw Myron standing near the large windows.

The State Attorney leaned his head forward and raised his glass in a silent salute, then returned to his conversation.

Nathaniel returned the gesture. He had been so anxious about tonight that only then had he realized Myron was speaking to Marielle and Lawrence. His tension ratcheted up a notch. Hearing his name, he turned to see Jason Krauss approaching.

"Patriots might have a pretty good year if the preseason is any indicator." Jason spoke with a smile.

Nathaniel shook his friend's hand, grateful to find someone he felt comfortable with. "Only if they get some players off the injured reserve."

Jason scanned the crowd. His gaze looked toward Myron and back to Nathaniel. "I hear rumors that congratulations are in order."

"They won't be rumors after tonight."

Myron met Nathaniel's gaze and jerked back his head, gesturing him over.

He nodded and clapped Jason on the shoulder. "Looks like I'm up. Excuse me."

"Good luck in the big leagues." Jason said. "Oh,

and if you talk to Val, tell her we're sorry about her dad."

Hearing Val's name, Nathaniel stopped, his body still. "Val's dad? What do you mean?"

"I thought you knew. Val's dad was diagnosed with colon cancer. She got a call at work and left for West Virginia right away."

Nathaniel's mouth went dry. "When was this?"

"Maybe a month ago. Lisa sure misses her."

Nathaniel left Jason and crossed the room, nodding and greeting people as he passed, but his mind was still on Val. He thought back to a conversation he'd had with Seth a few weeks earlier. His friend had acted strange, asking if he'd heard from Val and telling Nathaniel he should really check on her. Nathaniel had just chalked the suggestion up to Seth being nosy. He hadn't seen or heard from Val since the day of the garden party, and he'd thought making a clean break would be easier for both of them.

But by doing so, he hadn't been available for her when she needed him. What had happened? Was her father still alive? Had she moved to West Virginia permanently? What about Paris?

Norah Sutherland laid a hand on his arm, stopping him. "Nathaniel, this is such a big night. I'm so happy for you."

He thanked her and moved away. Seeing her brought back memories of the garden party, something he hadn't allowed himself to think of at all. An image tickled in his mind. Val had seemed strange after he'd returned from talking to Myron that evening. She'd acted distracted and anxious to leave. He'd even asked if someone had said something. He'd wondered if she was disappointed with him for considering the job when it would mean so much time away from his family, but that didn't seem like Val at all. She supported him in anything.

Nathaniel reached Myron and shook his hand.

Myron picked up a spoon and tapped it against his goblet, quieting the room. "Ladies and gentlemen, if I may have your attention. I know this announcement will come as no surprise to most of you, but I would like to present the newest member of my staff, a man whose extraordinary career I have followed for years. He will be a valuable addition to the State Attorney General's office as an advocate for the District of Massachusetts." Myron put his arm around Nathaniel's shoulders. "Please give your support to Nathaniel Cavanaugh."

The sound of polite applause filled the room. Many of those gathered raised their glasses and nodded their heads.

Nathaniel looked at the crowd. The elite of Boston. He'd moved in the same circles with these people his entire life, and he should feel some sort of closeness. He saw Marielle and Lawrence beaming and felt like a child who had done exactly what his teacher had asked. Though he knew their names, most of the people in the ballroom were strangers. The three people he cared about the most weren't even present to share the biggest moment of his career.

He pasted on a smile, thanking those that approached him to offer congratulations, but instead of feeling the measure of his accomplishment, he felt empty inside.

Marielle slid her hand into the crook of his elbow.

"Oh, Nathaniel. Clara would have been so proud tonight."

He looked down at her face—so like her daughter's. "You're right. She would have."

"Congratulations." Lawrence patted Nathaniel's other arm.

Marielle gave him a small tug, reclaiming his attention. "And when I think of where you could go from here. This is just the start of everything. If you make the right connections, no doubt you'll shoot straight to the top." She wagged her bony finger at him. "You mark my words. I'm just so thankful you saw the light and cut that low-brow person from your life before she could ruin all of this."

"Marielle…" Lawrence cleared his throat

"What do you mean?" Nathaniel's chest clenched.

"Nothing. She's just happy for you." Lawrence put his arm around her shoulders, turning her away.

Heart pounding, he leaned close. "Marielle, are you talking about Val?"

Frowning, she turned her head. "Well, really, Nathaniel. Can you imagine her at something like this with her 'y'alls' and short skirts? What would people think? We worked so hard to get you here, and she would have destroyed it."

"You said something to her, didn't you?" He spoke through gritted teeth as blood surged through his body. "At the Sutherland's garden party."

Marielle turned fully then crossed her arms and lowered her eyelids. "She needed to know what the stakes were. That it was your career on the line. And the way you were acting—like the poor lonely widower—you weren't in any condition to see things clearly. Not with all that cleavage right in front of you."

"Marielle!" Lawrence dropped open his mouth, and he glanced around.

A burning sensation attacked Nathaniel's gut. "You've overstepped, Marielle. My life and my relationships are not your business."

She pulled back her chin and barked a laugh. Any trace of politeness left her expression. "Relationship? Don't kid yourself. After all the work Clara did...all of us did to get you here, I couldn't let your hormones—"

Nathaniel spun before he could hear the rest of her sentence. He slammed down the champagne glass on a table, sloshing liquid over his hand, and ignoring people who tried to stop him along the way as he left the ballroom. He texted the driver and paced back and forth on the sidewalk while he waited.

So many thoughts fought for space in his head, focusing on only one took all his will. Marielle's words stunned him. He resented her implications Clara was the reason he'd been appointed to his job, but that wasn't the thing that bothered him the most. Her inferences about Val made him so angry his jaw hurt from clenching his teeth.

He was sick when he remembered how Val had acted that night and realized she wanted to leave, not to get away from him, but because of what Marielle had said. Val was worried about his reputation, worried that she would somehow ruin his career. If only she had told him. He would have...He would have what?

In the car, he dialed Seth's number.

Seth answered on the first ring. "You miss me, don't you?"

Nathaniel wasn't in the mood for Seth's

cheerfulness. "You knew about Val's father."

"Yeah, I knew. She called about a month ago to ask about cancer treatment options."

He tore loose his tie. "Why didn't you tell me?"

"I promised Val I wouldn't. She said you'd just try to help and she didn't want to take you away from work, something about ruining your political career. She didn't make a whole lot of sense. I agreed, though, not because I wanted to, but Val doesn't exactly take no for an answer."

He'd been right. Nathaniel clenched his teeth again as anger against his mother-in-law threatened to cloud his thoughts. "And her father?"

"He's doing better. They opted for surgery, and the surgeons think they got all the cancer. Val's down there taking care of him."

Of course she was. Of course she gave up her dream to take care of someone. That was Val. He didn't know what kind of insurance coal miners had, but he could bet Val paid for the medical bills with the money she'd saved for France.

He hung up and punched in Val's number, but she didn't answer. He knew she wouldn't.

****

That night, Nathaniel stood in Ruby's doorway watching her sleep. His gaze traveled around the room and stopped on her little table and tea set. He felt his stomach plummet. Hadn't he promised to have a tea party this weekend? Or was it last weekend? He stepped closer and, in the dim light, saw place tags for her dolls, written in her little-girl handwriting. He picked up one that said, "Daddy." His vision blurred.

A memory surfaced and, instead of pushing it away

178

as was his first instinct, he allowed all of the feelings it dredged up to wash over him. He was sixteen and had just pitched a no-hitter at his high school baseball game. The crowd cheered and chanted his name, and his teammates swarmed the mound, lifting him onto their shoulders. He looked around the crowd for the one person he'd asked to come—his dad. But he wasn't there. Bitter tears had prickled Nathaniel's teenage eyes, washing away the elation he'd felt a moment earlier.

His dad had told him later he'd had a late meeting he couldn't get out of.

Nathaniel had said he understood. And that night he'd promised himself he'd never do that to his kids. He'd always be present at events that were important to them. A wave of shame filled him, knowing he hadn't kept that promise to the sixteen-year-old boy on the pitcher's mound.

He thought of Val. How quickly she had left everything she'd worked for to return home and care for her dad. She'd given up her goal for what mattered most.

He looked back to the mass of dark hair on the pillow. He would give his children anything. They lived in an exclusive neighborhood, attended the best schools, owned every toy and gadget a child could ever want. But he hadn't given them the thing they wanted most. And it was the very thing he had longed for at their age.

How had he forgotten to give them a family?

****

The next morning, Nathaniel pushed back his shoulders as he stood outside the heavy wooden door of the Attorney General's office. He knocked and hearing an acknowledgement inside, he entered.

Myron grinned when he saw Nathaniel. "Glad to see you here so early." He spread his hand toward a chair in front of the desk.

Nathaniel shook his head. For just an instant, he felt a pang in his chest, but he had made up his mind and pressed on. He clasped his hands behind his back. "Sir, I apologize. I'm not able accept this position."

An hour later, Nathaniel left the courthouse. Once he got to his car, he again called Val, but she didn't answer. So, he placed a call to his assistant—even though she was no longer technically his assistant.

"Mr. Cavanaugh, the earliest flight to Charleston leaves later this afternoon with an overnight layover in Washington. The other flights I found would take just as long."

Nathaniel gritted his teeth. He might as well drive.

"But I did find a flight to Pittsburgh that takes off in an hour and a half. Then you'd just have a few hours' drive…"

"Book it." He steered his car in the other direction. "And a rental car too." He hung up and called his nanny to tell her his change of plans.

****

Nearly eight hours later, his GPS told him he was in Millford Creek. Nathaniel realized he had no idea how to find Val's house. He didn't have an address and when he'd searched a local directory on his phone, he couldn't find her or her family. He'd heard her talk about her trailer, and living in the holler, but he wasn't even sure what that meant.

He drove over the narrow road snaking through the

forest and passed a sign that said, "Welcome to Millford Creek." Finally, he saw houses between the trees and, after rounding a bend, arrived in the town. The street widened. He crossed railroad tracks and drove past a gas station, a pharmacy, and a building with a bell tower he assumed was the town hall. He decided that was the place to inquire about finding the McKinley's house.

He tried the door, but it was locked. A glance at his watch told him the time was nearly six-thirty. Would he need to locate a hotel and return in the morning? The idea didn't thrill him, and he felt a sense of urgency now that he was here. He needed to find Val.

Across the street, a group of men sat on chairs in front of the drugstore. Only one of them wore a shirt, and all had unkempt beards.

Nathaniel approached them with measured steps. "Good evening, I hoped you gentlemen could help me. Do any of you know where I might find the McKinley home?"

The men stared.

"You with the government?" One man asked, his eyes narrowing as he looked at Nathaniel's dark suit and tie.

The distrust in their expressions was obvious. Nathaniel should have thought this through better. And at least changed his clothes. "No. I'm actually a friend of Val's."

The man tipped forward his head and lowered his eyelids. He spit a brown stream on the sidewalk.

Nathaniel stepped back to keep it from splashing on his shoes. "Val worked for me this summer in Maine. I heard her father was sick, and I came down to…" *to what?* To fix everything? To offer support? Why had he come? Now wasn't the time to dwell on the thoughts, he'd second-guessed himself the entire way down here. All he knew is he needed to find her. To make sure she was all right. "I came down to check on her."

"Heard Val worked for a rich guy this summer," one of the men muttered.

The man who'd spoken first nodded. "Y'all gotta go down into the holler. Val's place is at the end of the road." He pointed back the way Nathaniel had come.

"Do you have an address? I'm not quite sure…"

"Follow the road back the way ya come. Turnoff's right past the union sign. You'll know you're there when you can't go no farther without landing in the crick."

"Thank you." Nathaniel hesitated, shook the men's hands then returned to his vehicle, flipped the car around, and headed back into the trees. He passed a rusted Miners' Union sign and looked for a turnoff. If he hadn't known the road was there, he'd have missed it. The path was nothing more than overgrown tire ruts leading off the main road.

He steered the car to the right and followed the road between hills and deeper into the wooded valley until it ended in front of a small trailer in a clearing. Clotheslines were strung across the yard. The sight of a green tank top with a cowboy boot silhouette fluttering alongside a pair of cut-off jeans made his heart jolt. He'd found the right place.

Braking to a stop, he parked next to a pickup truck and a small car on the side of the house. A large wooden porch was built onto the front of the trailer.

Nathaniel stepped out of the car, and two dogs emerged from beneath the porch and ran toward him, barking. He grabbed onto the door handle of the car, ready to jump back inside.

A man stepped out of the door. He yelled something that stopped the dogs then stood on the porch, crossing his arms.

Nathaniel felt his heart still beating fast. He watched the dogs from the side of his eye as he walked past and raised his hand in greeting. "Good evening. I'm Nathaniel Cavanaugh. Are you Mr. McKinley?"

The man remained silent.

He wore a ball cap and had a thick beard. Nathaniel searched his face for any resemblance to Val. "Sir, I'm a friend of Val's."

"You a lawyer?"

Nathaniel winced at the venom in the man's voice. Nothing would induce him to admit to being an attorney when two dogs were ready to spring toward him at a command. "Val worked for me this summer. I came to check on her. Are you her father?"

The man glanced back into the house and then, holding onto the rail, slowly walked down the stairs.

He had the look of a sturdy man who'd lost a great deal of weight in a short time, his skin was slightly yellowed, but he stood straight as he reached the bottom of the stairs, facing Nathaniel.

"Rex McKinley. I'm Val's daddy."

Nathaniel extended his hand and shook Rex's. His grip was strong, but Nathaniel could tell action took effort. He glanced at the house. "Is Val here?"

Rex nodded. "She just got home from the factory."

Nathaniel's heart skipped when he heard she was

so close. He looked past Rex through the screen door, but he couldn't see into the house.

Rex leaned heavily against the stair railing.

"And how are you feeling, sir?" Nathaniel wasn't sure if he should be assisting Val's father or not.

"I have good days. I'm not as sick as Val thinks. Not enough for her to drop everything to move back here and care for me like an inv'lid. 'Sides, doctor says it's all uphill from here, and I've got her brothers and sisters to help out." Rex lowered himself to the porch steps and jerked his head to the side, motioning for Nathaniel to join him. "But you know Val. She takes care of people. She's taken care of this family for fifteen years. That girl needs to be needed."

"I need her." Saying the words aloud sent a shock through him. Maybe he'd let down his guard because Val's father seemed so non-threatening. Or he could just be exhausted after traveling all day. He darted a look at Rex.

Val's father studied him for a moment. "Reckon you wouldn't be here otherwise." Rex pulled himself up and leaned against the rail as he climbed back up the stairs. "Val, come on outside."

****

When she heard her daddy call, Val dropped her dishtowel and hurried to the front door. *What is he doing outside?* He could overexert himself or even fall, and the doctor said he needed to take it easy.

Truthfully, she could tell he was improving. He complained more often about being cooped up in the house and insisted on doing more for himself, but Val was still worried. He'd had major surgery only a few weeks earlier.

Her daddy had been pushing her to get back to Boston, to get to Paris, but she wouldn't leave as long as she was still needed here. No dream was worth losing him.

She held open the door. "Come on back inside, Daddy. Supper's nearly—" She glanced at the bottom of the porch stairs and froze as her gaze met Nathaniel's. She felt her heart tumble at the sight, and she couldn't draw a breath. What was he doing here? How had he found her? *I'm gonna strangle Seth.* "Nathaniel, what in the world…"

Rex stepped close and placed his hand on her shoulder, looking her directly in the eye. "Val, you're so much like your momma, but that don't mean ya need to take her place." He glanced at Nathaniel and then back. "Y'all have some things to work out." He walked past her into the house.

Nathaniel climbed a few steps.

He still hadn't spoken. What was he thinking? Had he just come to check on her? If that was the case, he'd have to leave before anyone from the Attorney General's office found out where he was. Even as she thought of why he shouldn't be here, she felt her pulse race at the fact he'd come.

"Take a walk with me?" Nathaniel offered his hand.

With a cautious move, she slipped her hand in his. She could tell something was different in the way he looked at her, even his voice sounded different.

He turned, hesitated for a moment as he looked around the clearing, and finally led her down to the creek. When they reached the grassy bank, he turned and faced her. "Why didn't you answer my calls, and why didn't you tell me about your father? You shouldn't have had to deal with all this alone."

Val watched the running water. The feel of him, and the nearness. She was overwhelmed, and she didn't look into his eyes, knowing the sight would prevent her from focusing her thoughts. "I appreciate ya coming all the way down to check on me, but you really shouldn't have."

He lifted their joined hands to nudge her chin upward so their gazes met. "Why not? Isn't this what friends do?"

Val wanted to melt at his touch, wanted to lose herself in his eyes, and fall into his arms, but the pain that would follow wasn't worth the risk. She needed to guard her heart. And her frustration that she was the only one who realized what was at stake turned into annoyance. Stiffening, she released his hand and stepped back. "What if someone knew where you were? You need to think about your reputation."

Nathaniel shook his head. "Don't talk like that."

"You don't understand. This…" She waved her hand back and forth between them. "our…*relationship…*" she looked away, feeling her cheeks turn pink. "It could ruin everything for you. I'm not the kind of girl a man like you should be associated with." Val's throat constricted as she said the words, but she knew they were true. That painful fact had been brought up numerous times, but why did she have to be the one to spell it out?"

"You are the perfect girl for me to be with." He tipped his head to catch her gaze. "I didn't accept the job, Val."

She couldn't believe what she heard. What was he

saying? What had happened? Why would he pass up an opportunity like this? "But you'd worked so hard. I thought the position was your dream."

He lifted his shoulder in a shrug. "I thought so too, but the job wasn't what I wanted." Leaning forward, he took her hand again.

Val wondered if he could feel her pulse pounding. "I thought Paris was my dream," she whispered and glanced up. "But in the end, that wasn't what I wanted."

He pulled her toward him, sliding a hand around her waist. Cupping her chin, he lifted her face. "What's your dream, Val?"

Val's blood heated at his touch. She looked into his eyes, afraid of what she'd see, and at the same time afraid it wouldn't be there. Her heart felt like an out-of-control propeller. She shook her head.

"Tell me."

She wanted to tell him, wanted to scream it. Wanted to pull him closer and kiss him until she forgot her name, but the fear of his rejection was more than she could bear. "I can't."

He studied her face, moving his thumb over her jaw and sliding his hand to rest on the side of her neck. "A few months ago if you'd asked what my goals were, I would have told you I hoped for this job to be a springboard for my political and legal career. But I took a long look at my life and realized my goals weren't leading me in the direction I'd wanted. They weren't even *my* goals in the first place. The proposed job would give me even less time with my kids."

Nathaniel's arm tightened around her waist. "My dream is a family. This morning, I placed a call to Günter Jordan in Lobster Cove to see if he could use a partner. I'm hoping to buy Couthy Cottage and move north with the kids. Now the only thing missing from my dream is a woman who jumps in front of trolleys and bakes cornbread." His lips quirked. "You don't know where I could find someone like that, do you?"

"Do you need a nanny?" she whispered and lifted her gaze to his. Her fingers and toes tingled as she allowed a sliver of hope to penetrate into her chest.

He shook his head. His gaze held hers.

The expression in them made taking a breath difficult. She nibbled her lip.

"I need you, Val. My family wouldn't be complete otherwise."

Tears sprung into her eyes, and she felt as if her heart would explode.

Nathaniel brushed away the moisture on her cheeks. "But this will only work after you do your Paris internship."

"No, I'm not leaving y'all to—"

"I wouldn't even consider letting you go alone. The kids and I would be completely happy to spend the winter in Paris while you study. If you'd consider bringing them along for our honeymoon?"

Val pressed her hands against his cheeks and pulled his face to hers, meeting his lips as heat burst in her chest.

His lips moved over hers, his kiss deepening, and he pressed her against him tightly. His kisses, his touch, his words filled the empty places in her heart, and Val sighed, knowing she'd found where she belonged.

Epilogue

Nathaniel stood in the shade of the Lobster Cove Post Office watching the woman walking down First Street toward him. A spring wind blew the smell of blossoms, giving him hope the long Maine winter was finally over.

She wore a nice pair of slacks, colorful scarf, and designer shoes. Walking confidently, she shook her hair out of her face as the sea wind blew it. After glancing at the pedestrians, she veered away from the crowded sidewalk, stepping off the curb with a confident stride.

His heart flew into his throat. "Val!"

Val looked up.

Nathaniel rushed toward her. He took her arm and pulled her out of the street. "You didn't even look to see if the trolley was coming."

She smiled, showing the dimples in her cheeks. "Calm down. I was barely in the gutter. Don't be such a worrywart."

"Someone's got to look out for my wife." He pulled her into his arms and kissed her soundly. Her swollen tummy pressed against him. He took her hand and they strolled into the park.

"Did you pick up Ruby from school on time? You know how she gets when we're late."

He shook his head and chuckled. *Now who is the worrywart?* "I picked her up on time, just like I do every Tuesday and Thursday afternoon while you're at the gallery. I'm sure Mrs. Spencer is at this very moment feeding the children one of her delicious meals."

"What a good daddy you are." She squeezed his hand.

"Of course I am. Now how was the gallery today?"

"Wonderful, as usual. I sold one of Jane Nash's watercolors. But I have to say, The Venus Gallery isn't the same without the Copeland."

"I like it better in its new home at the cottage, don't you?"

She rested her head on his shoulder for just a moment. "I most certainly do. And I can't imagine any woman ever received a more thoughtful wedding gift."

They reached Nathaniel's car. He let Val inside and climbed in behind the steering wheel, turning the key. He shifted the car into gear and lifted Val's hand, holding it between the seats as he drove.

"How was work today with Günter?" Val asked.

"Good, we met with a few new clients and finalized necessary paperwork."

"I hope you have some plans for supper. I'm starving." She placed a hand on her stomach and rubbed a circle.

"No more horrific pregnancy cravings, if I hear you talking about squirrels and gravy again…" His stomach turned over at the thought.

"No, I'm not craving anything in particular. How about a hamburger or a lobster roll?"

He brushed his lips across her knuckles, loving that he could still make his wife shiver with such a small action. "Or what if we head home and put the kids in bed? I've got a craving myself for something sweet and Southern."

"We'll have to stop at the grocery mart—" Val began.

"Oh, you thought I meant food." He opened his eyes wide in an expression of innocence.

Val pulled her hand from his and gave him a playful swat.

Darkness had fallen by the time they finished dinner and left Lobster Cove to drive back to the cottage.

Val leaned her elbow on the armrest and laid her head against his shoulder. "I sure do love you, Mr. Cavanaugh."

"I love you too, Mrs. Cavanaugh."

He turned off the cliff road and drove through the trees until he saw the lights burning in the windows. *Not forgotten.* A warm feeling of contentment rolled over him as he glanced at the woman at his side. Val had given him a family. He was finally home.

A word about the author...

Jennifer Moore is a passionate reader and writer of all things romance due to the need to balance the rest of her world that includes a perpetually traveling husband and four active sons, who create heaps of laundry that is anything but romantic. She suffers from an unhealthy addiction to 18th and 19th century military history and literature. Jennifer has a B.A. in Linguistics from the University of Utah and is a Guitar Hero champion. She lives in northern Utah with her family, but most of the time wishes she was on board a frigate during the Age of Sail.

authorjmoore.com

Another Title by the Author
The Sheik's Ruby